CYNTHIA HICKEY

Deadly Greenhouse Gases

A Shady Acres Mystery, Book 5

By Cynthia Hickey

1

"*Y*our father died on a day like this."

"Yes, Mom, I know." I glanced out the window of Shady Acres's welcome center.

The trees had lost their autumn foliage and now stretched their skeletal branches to a cold January sky. The winter sun sparkled off the engagement ring my fiancé, Heath, had given me at Christmas. Normally, the sight brightened my day, but not today. A cloud shadowed the day this time every year.

"Dad died exactly five years ago today." Shot in the line of duty during a routine traffic stop where the shooter sped from the scene before backup arrived. I often wondered whether the unsolved crime of his death might be the reason I so easily jumped into trying to solve mysteries.

"I think he would like Bob, don't you?" She glanced up from her receptionist desk.

I gave a sad smile. "They would have been poker buddies.

Bob Satchett held a poker game every Friday night in his cottage. I was a regular attendee. I wasn't sure Dad would have approved, but I was his little girl. Other than a frown, he wouldn't have said a derogatory word.

"How is the electricity coming in the greenhouse?"

"Not well." I sighed. "Alice bought a generator. She said the ancient lights are too much of a drain on the main system."

Alice, the manager of Shady Acres, had bought a used generator. I hated the noisy, smelly thing. Alice's secondary reason for the ancient monster was that corporate hadn't approved the work order and Heath wasn't certified to do the repairs.

Through the window, I watched as Scott Cline unloaded boxes onto a dolly and wheeled them inside. "Delivery, Mrs. Hart." He grinned, stacking the boxes next to her desk. "A few heavy ones."

"Those would be the copy paper. Thank you. Have a cookie or two, there on the sideboard." Mom pulled a box cutter from her top drawer and started cutting.

"How are you Scott?" I smiled.

"Just fine Shelby." His eyes didn't hold the usual glitter. "It's a bit cold for driving around in a truck without doors."

"I feel the same way on the golf cart, although it doesn't go over fifteen miles per hour. Speaking of, I'd better get to work. The herbs won't plant themselves." I said my goodbyes and headed for the greenhouse.

Lined up in a neat row were seedlings ready to be planted. In warm weather, I set them right into the garden. But January left a frost that would kill the fledgling plants. On the other side of the glass wall the generator rumbled like an awoken beast out for blood. The racket would give me a headache for sure.

Being the anniversary of Dad's death, I found it hard to concentrate. All I could think of was his partner showing up at our door with the bad news. Mom had collapsed. I sat on the sofa, stunned, while Donald, my then fiancé, paced the living room.

"Hello, gorgeous." Heath entered, a dozen red roses in his hand. "I thought you could use these today. Ida told me what day it was."

Tears sprang to my eyes. "I don't deserve you." I really didn't. Kindness seeped from my Chris Hemsworth lookalike fiancé. He always thought of others before himself, and while he didn't always like the idea, he backed me up when I set off to find a killer. I buried my face in the flowers then raised my head for a kiss.

He obliged, then pulled me close for a hug. "How about you work later and let's take a walk?"

"That sounds wonderful. I'd like to stop by my place and put these in water first."

Heath escorted me home where I cut a couple of inches off the stems and put the flowers into a crystal vase before setting them in the center of my table. "I wish I had fresh flowers every day. They bring a house alive."

"I'll do my best." Heath wrapped his arms around me from behind and nuzzled my neck.

"Don't be silly." I giggled. "In the warm months I have a garden full of flowers. I just need to cut a few."

"Every day? There'll be no blooms left." He turned

me, kissed me, and took my hand to lead me outside for our walk. "I'll take care of the days when you have no flowers, even if it's a single rose."

I had the best guy in the world. Sad how reluctant I was to get engaged. But, after having been left at the altar, love wasn't something I thought was real.

Just inside the maze, I spotted Grandma and her fiancé, Ted, in a hot and heavy kissing session. "Doesn't she realize she's in her sixties? She acts more like sixteen."

"Let her enjoy life. I think it's cute. In fact, we could probably learn something from those two."

I laughed and linked my arm with his. "I like us the way we are."

Grandma spotted us. "Yoo hoo! We're over here."

I sighed and strolled toward her. "We saw you."

"Were you looking for me?"

"No, just out for a walk before I replant some herbs."

"I have a great idea for this weekend's community get-together."

"Good, because I have nothing."

As not only the gardener, I was also the event coordinator of Shady Acres and was in charge of weekly gatherings. I've tried talking Alice into a monthly event, instead, but she said the residents look forward the parties.

"Ted and I will get married. Everyone will be there!"

I had not expected that. A 20s party, a murder mystery, plenty of things besides a wedding. "Why so sudden?"

"I'm not pregnant if that's what you're worried

about."

I opened and shut my mouth several times then glanced at Heath for help. The things that came out of my grandmother's mouth often left me speechless.

"I think that's wonderful," he said, his eyes twinkling. "It's kind of cold, but the fountain is still a beautiful spot."

Not to mention it had been a crime scene not once, but twice, in the past few months. "Do you want your wedding shadowed by murder?" I shook my head. "We can fix the hall up pretty."

"No, I like the idea of the mystique of our infamous fountain. In fact, I want a Winter Wonderland wedding. We'll rent a snow machine, string white sparkling lights over every surface. The reception can be in the hall." Grandma caressed Ted's cheek. "Teddy is in full agreement, right sweetie?"

"I know better than to argue with you. Shelby, we'll need a lot of white roses. I want Ida to have whatever she wants."

"I know where to find them." We'd all freeze our patooties off, but it did promise to be beautiful. "I'd better head to work and place that call for roses." I stood on tiptoes and gave Heath a quick kiss.

"I'll see what else they want done for this weekend and meet up with you later."

I shoved my hands in the pockets of my coat and headed back to the greenhouse. Once there, I placed a call on the installed phone for an outrageously expensive amount of white roses. The poor girl on the other end had to repeat the order back to me several times in order to be heard over the noise of the generator.

I'd almost rather work without electricity than put up with the awful noise. I picked up a tomato plant in a dissolvable carton and set it into the dirt of a planter. Soon, I had a whole row of lovely plants that would yield fresh tomatoes. I then moved to basil.

My eyelids grew heavy. I needed a nap. After surveying the amount of work left to do, I decided against the guilty pleasure and kept working.

I spotted Heath smiling at me from the other side of the wall. I lifted a heavy hand and…collapsed in a heap in on the dirt floor.

When I opened my eyes, I was lying on the ground outside, a worried Heath leaning over me. "Somebody call an ambulance."

"I'm fine." I tried to sit. Nausea and a pounding headache prevented me from getting up.

"I called." Mom leaned over me and held up two fingers. "How many?"

"Two." I pushed her hand away. "I didn't hit my head. I just fainted, or something."

"You don't faint." She planted hands on her hips. "Our people never faint."

"I did once," Grandma said.

"No, you didn't." Mom glared. "You passed out from too much wine."

"Nonsense." Grandma bent over me and patted my cheek. "You look pale."

Please, God, where was the ambulance?

"Scott!" Mom waved a hand. "Would you please stand in the parking lot and direct the paramedics when they arrive."

I couldn't see him, but he must have agreed, because Mom looked satisfied. My question was…why was he still there and not doing his job? "Help me sit up." I held up a hand. "Where's Heath?"

"I'm here. I turned off the generator and opened the doors of the greenhouse."

"Why?" I glanced into his face, lacking its normal kindness.

"Because someone hooked up a hose to the inside of the greenhouse. You've been poisoned with carbon monoxide, is my guess."

"Don't jump to conclusions." Ted marched to the back of the building. Being a retired police officer, he couldn't help but take charge when something happened. He returned a few minutes later. "Yep, Heath is right. We'll have to wait for Seth, who is on his way, but that generator tried to kill you."

"Seriously? It's an inanimate object. A living person tried to kill me." Who wanted me dead this time? I hadn't been involved in a death since before Christmas. That was weeks ago. Those hadn't been aimed at me. Not until I'd gotten close to the killer, anyway. "Why would someone want to kill me?" I glanced at all their worried faces.

"Honey," Heath squatted next to me. "Who wouldn't want to? Think about it. You've been the reason for murderers to either die themselves or be put behind bars. Those killers obviously had families."

"You're saying this was revenge? Why couldn't it have been an accident? Someone messing with the generator that had no idea of the dangers?"

He cocked his head, looking at me with pity. "You're smarter than that. The residents of Shady Acres wouldn't be caught dead getting their hands dirty."

"Don't say dead." I laid back on the ground.

Someone wanted me dead. What a way to start off the New Year. "I almost died on the same day as my father."

2

Seth, accompanied by a young rookie cop, marched down the walkway. "Of course, it has to be Shelby in the middle of things." He not only took Ted's place as the officer I annoyed the most, but was also the boyfriend of my best friend, Cheryl Leroix, which sometimes made life complicated.

"Nice to see you, too." I grinned. "I promise I've done nothing but plant herbs."

"Hmm hmm." He headed straight for Heath.

Soon, the two were deep in conversation and heading around to the back of the greenhouse. I refused to be left out of my almost murder. I struggled to my feet and shuffled after them.

"You should stay put until the paramedics arrive." Officer Wayman, by the name on his shirt, crossed his arms.

"You silly man," Grandma said, following me.

"You'll learn soon enough, poor thing, how the women in this family work." We pushed past him.

"Ma'am." A paramedic jogged toward me. "We need to give you oxygen."

"As long as I can hear what's going on then feel free." Secretly, I was glad for the oxygen. Every breath was a struggle.

Seth eyed the hose from the generator to the greenhouse. Duct tape connected one end of a cut off water hose to the generator and another into a hole cut into one of the glass panes. Seeing the evidence that the carbon monoxide was not an accident made my legs weak. I sagged against the paramedic.

The man lowered me to the ground. "I'll fetch a gurney."

I waved off his suggestion. I'd be fine in a little bit.

"Shelby Hart, you're lucky Heath showed up when he did," Seth said, standing from his squatted position. "A few minutes more and we'd be planning your funeral. So, who did you make mad this time?"

I shrugged rather than remove the oxygen mask and answer him. Especially since I had no answer to give.

"Yep, that was a close call." Grandma put a hand on my shoulder. "Glad whoever tried didn't succeed." She leaned down and whispered in my ear. "We'll catch the culprit, just like always."

I'd really wanted to hang up my gumshoeing shoes. It didn't appear this was the year to do so. I glanced around the crowd of spectators. Everyone was there. Bob Satchett, Mom's boyfriend, Birdie Sorenson, her hair died a bright yellow this time, Hattie Black, Scott Cline, and a host of others. All friends and residents. Had the would-be murderer done the deed and run, or could one of these curious onlookers have decided the world would be better off without me?

Tears pricked my eyes. Surely it wasn't one of my friends? I worked hard to keep Shady Acres a beautiful place to live. Many of them had actually come to me at one time or another to help them find a killer or a thief. Knowing how hard I worked on their behalf should make them love me, right?

"Are you in pain, ma'am?" The paramedic peered into my face.

I shook my head. What hurt me couldn't be soothed with oxygen or medicine. What a ninny? Of course the attempted murderer wasn't one of these onlookers.

The paramedic removed the oxygen mask. "Stay seated. I'll check your vitals in a few minutes. I really think you should go to the hospital for evaluation."

"Not necessary. I'm feeling much better. Heath!"

My love whipped around, then rushed to my side. "What's wrong? Are you all right?"

"Can you hold me for a minute?"

"Oh, darling." He wrapped me in his arms and led me to a bench where he pulled me onto his lap. "It's gotten to you, hasn't it?"

"Yes." I rested my cheek on his chest. "It's one thing to go after someone who killed another, but to go after the person who wants me dead is…scary."

His chest rumbled. "Only you would categorize catching killers."

"This one is personal."

"You make them all personal at some point."

I knew he wasn't a fan of my need to seek justice, but sweet man that he was, he supported me. He also helped me, more to try and keep me safe than actually helping on the hunt, I guessed. Helping catch killers was something I did for my father. I wasn't ready to stop.

"I'll start nosing around tomorrow. I wouldn't want the case to go cold," I said.

"For crying out loud, Shelby Hart!" Seth glared. "Let me do my job, please."

"Someone tried to kill me."

"I'm aware of that. Try sitting this one out. I might surprise you and actually catch the culprit on my own." He shook his head and went to converse with Officer Wayman.

"You'd think he'd know better." Ted stood next to us and crossed his arms. "But, he'll have to learn the hard way, same as I did."

"It's taking him longer to get through his head that I won't sit back and do nothing," I said.

"He's young. His head is harder."

I doubted that. It was a toss-up in my opinion.

~

By the time the paramedics reluctantly gave me a clean bill of health and my greenhouse was roped off with yellow crime scene tape, the bell for lunch rang. Where had Alice been during the uproar? Usually, she was right in the thick of things.

I left Heath and the others at our usual table and headed for Alice's office. I knocked, then entered when summoned.

She sat behind her desk, eyes red from crying. "Oh, good. You're alive."

I frowned. "Uh, how did you know I was in danger?"

"Your mother called me." She wiped her eyes with

a Kleenex. "Corporate is getting tired of the murders around here. They seem to think it's my fault. I tried telling them we were at full capacity, probably because of the thrill of living in such a beautiful, but dangerous place. Oh, Shelby, they want to replace me."

"With who?"

She shrugged. "I don't know and I don't care."

"Can you change their minds?"

"Maybe."

We weren't the best of friends, but I'd get a petition signed by everyone. Alice might be bossy and opinionated, but she was as much a part of Shady Acres as the crazy maze at the end of the property or our resident vampire, Leroy Manning, a man allergic to the sun. "Have you eaten? Would you like me to bring you a plate?"

"I'm not hungry. How can you think I could eat at a time like this? They're making their decision by the end of the week!"

Oh. Grandma's wedding. "By the way...my grandmother wants to get married on Saturday by the fountain."

"I probably won't be here to see it happen. Do whatever you want." She put her head in her hands. "Please go."

Not one of my best days. Heart heavy, I joined the others and explained Alice's predicament.

"Here." Grandma reached into her cavernous canary yellow bag and pulled out a notepad. "Go around the room and get signatures right now. We cannot let this happen. Why, look at this place. Since Alice had the brains to hire you as gardener to pretty the place up and help her find ways to draw in residents, we're full. That has to account for something."

"Yeah, like Shelby should be manager. Most of the improvements were her idea in the first place," Mom said. "She did the physical labor and the brain work."

"All good managers delegate," I said. "The reason Corporate is upset is because of the killings, or so Alice says. Making me manager wouldn't change that. Plus, I'd hate being stuck behind a desk."

I wrote on the top of the paper what the petition was for and sent Grandma around to work her charm. "I think I'm going to lay down after lunch," I said. "Almost dying takes a lot out of a person."

"I think that's a great idea." Mom patted my hand. "Take a nap, then reconsider finding out who is responsible. Follow Seth's advice. My heart can't take it. Oh, and your grandmother canceled her wedding plans."

"The roses!" I dug my cellphone from my pocket and quickly canceled the order. Once I saved myself a few hundred dollars, I glanced at Mom. "Why did she cancel?"

"She said the two of you were going to be too busy for a wedding. You created a monster, Shelby, the first time you let her help you solve a crime. What kind of woman cancels a wedding because she'd rather catch a killer?" Mom's eyes were wide. "A crazy one, that's what kind. Back to the subject of manager...see how you delegated the job of getting the petition signed? You're a natural."

That made me a chip off the ol' Ida block in regards to being crazy. As for manager, I didn't want the job. After a lunch of potato soup and bread, I headed to my cottage for the much needed nap. Heath promised to check on me in an hour. If I was sleeping, he'd leave me be. In the meantime, he and Grandma would make sure they got every single Shady Acre resident to sign the petition to keep Alice as manager.

I drifted to sleep within seconds of laying my head on my pillow. I wasn't sure what time it was when a loud noise woke me. I bolted upright. The curtains at my window fluttered with the winter breeze. "What the heck?"

I climbed from bed. Glass crunched under my bare feet. A piece jabbed into the ball of my foot. I hissed and tip-toed gingerly to the center of my room. Lying there was the head of a ceramic garden gnome. I blinked, then stared. Who would behead a gnome?

Heath barged into the room and skid to a halt. "What happened?"

I pointed and sat on the edge of the mattress to pull out the sliver of glass. "Someone doesn't like garden gnomes, I guess."

"There's a note stuck inside its head." He pulled out a rolled piece of paper and read: "Watch your back. Payment is due."

"What does that mean?" I hopped into the bathroom for the peroxide. "I don't owe anyone anything." Even my Volkswagon was paid off. Rent at Shady Acres was included in my salary. I was a rare American who lived debt free.

"This has to be from the person who tried to gas you." Heath hefted me onto the sink and took over ministrations of my foot. "It has to be someone from Shady Acres."

"But why? We're all friends here." I'd never harmed any of them.

CYNTHIA HICKEY

"That's what we need to find out." He slapped a band-aid on my foot. "I've got to call Seth. Can you make it to the livingroom?"

I nodded. "I'll walk on my heels."

While he left to make his phone call, I hobbled to the sofa and plopped down. What debt? I rested my head against the back of the seat. Had I wronged someone unknowingly? There was no other explanation. I'd have to question the residents and see who held a grudge against me. If I struck out, I'd think deeper, harder, about a debt I might owe.

"Seth is on his way." Heath sat next to me. "Do you need anything? It's almost time for supper."

"I am hungry. I didn't have much of an appetite at lunch." We both knew I usually had quite the healthy appetite despite my petite size. I sighed. "I can't think of any debt I owe, much less one large enough to kill me over."

"We'll find out who's behind this."

Grandma barged through the front door and handed me the signed petition. "Everyone signed. I told them they wouldn't be invited to my wedding if they didn't." She looked very pleased with herself. "I'm not adverse to a bit of bribery now and again. So…we'll need an open bar when we have the reception."

I glanced at Heath. We both burst into laughter.

"What?" Grandma frowned.

"You're something else," I said.

"Why is there a band-aid on your foot?" She cocked her head.

"Someone threw a gnome head through my bedroom window and I stepped on the glass." I explained about the note.

"Why, that's easy. My guess is it's a relative of one of the killers from our previous escapades. That's the only option that makes sense." She rubbed her hands together. "This will be the best murder mystery yet."

"Don't you ever tire of the danger?" I clutched a throw pillow to my chest.

"Why would I? God willing, I have another twenty or thirty years left of my life. Might as well live adventurously. We aren't guaranteed tomorrow, you know?"

"I know." Still, the constant chasing after danger was taking its toll on me. Then, there came the adrenaline rush of bringing a killer to justice. I was feeling like pulled taffy.

3

*T*he next morning, instead of enjoying my made-to-order omelet, I found myself studying each resident who entered the door of the dining hall. One of them wanted to kill me. The thought sent my heart to the pit of my stomach.

I'd arrived at Shady Acres early last summer with a broken heart. Still, I'd settled right in despite finding a dead body my first day. I honestly thought these people had grown to love me as much as I loved them.

"Cheer up, darlin'." Grandma sat next to me, a fluted glass of what I suspected was a mimosa. "You're alive and breathing."

"It hurts to think someone hates me so much they want me dead." I blinked back tears.

"Don't forget those who love you." She patted my hand. "Now, step away from the pity party and start thinking. Who would hold a grudge against you? Start with those you brought to justice. Let's go with my idea of their family being a little ticked off."

"Harry Weasley was the first, then Alan Barker, Susan Hall, and Sasha Woodrow. Do you really think one of them is the debt I owe? What about the victims?"

She shook her head. "No, I think that would be on the heads of the police. You couldn't save them, but you did have an active hand in the death or capture of the four you mentioned."

I pushed my omelet around my plate. It made sense. When I finished work for the day, I do some research on these names and see whether any had ties to someone at Shady Acres. Harry Weasley would be the hardest because he'd been her under the Witness Protection Act. But, I could search his real name…Harvey Weston.

Relieved to have a game plan, I set to eating with my usual gusto. Investigating took a lot of energy out of a person. When I'd finished, I went to visit Mom at her desk.

I wrote down the names of the people I'd decided to start my investigation with and handed it to her. "Could you please search all resident files for any mention of these names?"

"Yes, but give me a few days. It won't be quick." She stuffed the list under her desk blotter. "I assume you're going to be doing research of your own."

"Of course. But things move faster with two people. I'll be online later this evening. Thanks, Mom." I smiled, knowing how much she hated me getting involved. I also knew she'd help me hoping to lessen the danger to her only child.

"I don't understand how a well-behaved child grew into such an adventure seeking adult. You never gave me a moment of despair until you moved here."

"I think I finally decided to take control of my own life. After Donald jilted me, well, I wasn't going to allow anyone to dictate what I should and should not do."

She raised worried eyes. "But does it have to mean constant danger?"

I stepped around the desk to give her a hug. "I can't sit back when someone tried to kill me. All I can do is find them as quickly as possible."

"And I'll do what I can to help." She caressed my cheek. "Now get to work."

Taking her advice, I headed for the greenhouse, stopping when I caught sight of the crime scene tape surrounding the building. How was I supposed to plant my herbs?

Heart pounding in my throat, I circled the greenhouse, relieved to see the generator was no longer hooked up and providing electricity or poisonous gas. I went back to the front and slipped under the tape. There was enough sunlight to provide light to work by, although it would be a might chilly. I dug a paper mask, the type doctors wore in surgery, from a box on a shelf and hooked it over my nose for good measure. I wasn't taking any more chances with toxic fumes.

By lunchtime, I had all my herb seedlings replanted and was starving. Feeling quite pleased with myself, I shoved open the greenhouse door and knocked Seth back a few feet. "I'm sorry. I didn't see you."

He rubbed his nose. "Imagine my surprise to see you working in a crime scene."

"I have a job to do. Besides, I'm working on a suspect list." I rattled off the names. "Grandma and I are going with the idea that someone connected to these four tried to gas me."

"It's a good start." He tilted his head. "I don't think you should wander around alone until we catch this perp."

"No one can leave behind their own work to babysit me." I removed the mask and shoved it into my pocket.

"Since you have Ida running around like a headless chicken interrogating everyone, maybe you can keep her close. She's interfering with my investigation. She's going to tip off the would-be killer." His eyes narrowed. "I'd hate to arrest her again."

"Don't threaten me with arrest. It didn't work out so well the last time." I wrapped my arms tight around my middle trying to ward off the January cold. "We all know you won't risk upsetting Cheryl again unless it's for something really big."

"I never should have fallen for the best friend of a lunatic."

I laughed and headed for the golf cart. "Silly man." I climbed into the seat and headed for the dining hall.

Sure enough, Grandma was circling the tables, clipboard in hand, barking out questions. Poor Bob was the object of her intense investigation at the moment. "If you're going to date my daughter, I must clear you of all suspicion."

"Why would I want to kill the daughter of the woman I love?" Bob shook his head. "Besides, if Shelby dies, I'll never have a chance to win back all the money I've lost to her in poker."

"Ah ha! You clearly have a motive."

I took her arm and dragged her into a corner. "Try to be more subtle, please. Seth has requested that you be my…bodyguard." I forced out the word. I loved her dearly, but having her around twenty-four seven would be torture.

Her eyes widened. "Really? That's an important job. I'll go get my gun and Tazor. Don't go anywhere. Oh, and I'll need to pack a few articles of clothing. Unless you're willing to come to my place?"

I shook my head.

"Very well. Stay here where everyone can see you." She fairly skipped from the building.

"That's the craziest thing I've ever heard." Alice stepped beside me. "You'll want to kill yourself in two days."

"I need to keep her from ruining Seth's investigation."

"You mean you want to keep an eye on her for your own snooping."

I shrugged. "Yeah. So, any news from corporate? Mom faxed over the petition yesterday."

She grinned. "They're keeping me for now. I'm still the manager until they evaluate again next January."

"That's good news." I clapped a hand on her shoulder and headed for the buffet once I spotted Heath.

His eyes widened after hearing Seth's request, then he burst out laughing. "Poor Shelby."

"Poor both of us. There goes any privacy we managed to carve out for ourselves." Which was precious little living in such a nosy place as Shady Acres.

"Right. Well, we'll have to be more creative. The maze makes a good snuggle place." His eyes twinkled.

"Maybe when it isn't forty degrees outside." I smiled and grabbed a chicken salad sandwich and a bowl of tomato soup before joining Mom and Bob at our community table. The round table for ten was filling out as our friends and family grew.

"Poker tomorrow night?" Bob asked.

"Wouldn't miss it," I replied. "I need to recoup my Christmas expenses by taking more of your money."

"Very funny, little girl. Your luck has to change sometime."

I sincerely hoped not, and I wasn't talking about poker. "We'll see."

"What's got you down in the mouth?" He pointed his fork at me. "We'll find out who's bothering you, mark my words. Your poker buddies won't let you down. We'll come up with a plan tomorrow night. Before you start thinking one of us is out to get you, well, just shove that thought right out of your mind. Wouldn't ever happen Miss Chicken Legs."

"Chicken legs?" My eyes widened. "When did you start calling me that?"

"First time I saw you in shorts." He laughed and stood, gathering his plate and utensils. "Tomorrow night, seven o'clock sharp, bring cookies."

Maybe the kitchen would whip me up a batch. Joyce and I were becoming quite close after I proved her innocence a few months ago. Since Grandma hadn't returned, Mom didn't show up, and Heath got stopped by Alice, I wolfed down my lunch then went to the kitchen.

"Feel like making cookies?" I grinned. "A variety? Maybe two dozen?"

"Girl, you're killing me." Joyce threw a wooden

spoon into a sink of soapy water. Suds splashed onto the floor. "I guess this is personal, am I right?"

"Yes. I'll pick them up right before seven tomorrow night."

"Poker." She rolled her eyes. "Bob already hit me up for buffalo wings and potato wedges. I should charge extra."

"I'll gladly pay."

She smiled. "You're probably the only one who would offer. Glad you didn't die. The cookies will be ready on time."

"Thank you." I gave her a quick one-armed hug and returned to the chilly outdoors.

Heath and Alice stopped me right outside.

"Shelby, I need some winter flowers delivered to room 301 in the main building. The resident there is recovering from surgery." Alice tapped a pen against a bright yellow clipboard. "I'm sure you can accommodate, right?"

"I don't grow a lot of flowers in the greenhouse this time of year. Can't you order some?" Seriously, the woman had no clue.

"I'm much too busy. If you can't get some of our own, then order some and make them look like we grew them. This woman is a very prestigious resident, Shelby. If we keep her happy, she'll tell her friends, and soon we'll have a waiting list." Her face fell. "The way people die around here, the waiting won't take long."

"Look, Alice. I've been very willing to do anything you ask of me." I planted my fists on my hips. "But some things need to be done by the manager. Go order the flowers yourself." I climbed into my golf cart and sped away at a whopping ten miles per hour toward the main building.

Oh, that felt good. I knew I'd feel a bit of guilt once I thought about it, but if Alice wanted to be the manager, then she needed to stop pushing all of her duties off on me. Somethings were her job and her job only. Like customer service, so to speak.

My top job was staying alive.

"I'm back." Grandma rushed into the reception room, her ginormous canary yellow bag on her shoulder. Every good or evil person within a mile would see her coming. "I have all my crime fighting tools. What's first?"

4

"*O*h, Teddy." Grandma leaned over Ted's shoulder and looked at his poker hand. "What a lovely family you have there."

Everyone groaned and tossed down their cards before glaring at me.

"What?" I glanced around the table. "Seth ordered protection. Grandma is it."

"For who?" Bob glared. "You or the would-be killer?"

"Ida, go sit on the sofa and look pretty," Ted said, waving her away. "You can't give away my hand like that."

"I was trying to speak in code, dear." She hmmphed and plopped on the sofa.

"That was cruel." I took the cards from Ted and shuffled since it was my turn to deal. "You were condescending and demeaning."

"I had a winning hand!" He frowned. "This is why women don't belong in poker…or investigating crimes."

Rolling my eyes, I set the deck of cards down while the other guys looked on. "If you have something to say, Ted, then say it. Stop pussy footing around the issue."

"Fine." He folded his hands on the table. "When I was still active law enforcement, putting up with your interfering was bad enough. Now, that is Seth's problem. But now that I'm about to marry Ida, and become a step-grandfather to you, I don't like the thought of either one of you in danger. I can't sleep at night. This foolish idea of making Ida your bodyguard sent me over the top!"

"That was Seth's idea because Grandma was…well, not being very subtle about snooping." I knew his attitude had nothing to do with poker.

"I'm right here," Grandma said. "No need to pretend like I'm not."

"See?" Ted pointed. "She doesn't understand."

"I understand plenty." She stood and sashayed over to him, wrapping her arms around his neck and kissing his ear. "You care for us. That scares you. But, honey, nothing is going to change."

"I know." He sighed and put his hand over hers. "I'm sorry for my unkind words."

"You can make it up to me with jewelry." She winked at me then returned to the sofa.

Leroy Manning nodded. "I realize that I may miss a lot by not stepping outside my cottage during daylight hours, but there is a lot that happens at night." He held up a hand at my questioning look. "No, I didn't see who hooked the hose up to your greenhouse. I think that happened in broad daylight. I can promise to keep an eye out and watch your cottage when honest people should be sleeping."

"That will make me feel a lot better," Heath said.

"I appreciate it, too, Leroy." I resumed shuffling. "Question is…how do I know one of you seated at this table didn't try to kill me?" I raised my eyes to see shocked looks on their faces. "I'd hate to think so, but it has to be someone from Shady Acres. Someone who thinks I owe them something. Maybe I angered one of you without realizing so."

Bob slapped his hand flat on the table. "Don't be ridiculous. There isn't a man in this room that wouldn't die for you, girl. We all look at you as our daughter. It hurts me deeply that you would entertain such a dumb idea."

"I'm sorry. No one else would have a reason to hate me." I sniffed.

"Lots of people do," Harold Ball said. "You're nosy, opinionated, and have a knack for putting away the bad guy. Bob is right, though. Everyone in this room loves you. What do you want us to do? We're here to help."

My heart swelled at the same time my shoulders slumped. "I have no idea. I'm drawing a blank." Unfortunately, I might not be able to do anything until my would-be assassin tries again. "I'll be doing some research on the computer, but that's about it. I'm looking to see who might have ties with those I've helped put behind bars."

"I can help with that." Ted flashed a grin. "I have resources you don't. You keep making this a beautiful place and let us find the bad guy."

I sighed. "You're being patronizing again."

"Sorry. Can't help myself."

I dealt the cards, and laughed as the groan from Ted signified he had nowhere near as good a hand as the last round. Instead, I won with a full house, Jack high. By the end of the night, while not exactly 'cleaning-up', I left forty dollars richer.

"I can't believe your luck," Heath said as we strolled along the flagstone walkway toward my cottage.

"Skill, sweetie. Skill."

He laughed and put an arm around my shoulder, drawing me close to his side. "Sure, it is. That, and the fact that every man back there is a tiny bit in love with you."

"Oh, stop. They're all old enough to be my father."

"So?" he gave me a squeeze.

I chuckled and nudged his shoulder. "Want a cup of coffee?" I glanced over my shoulder to where Grandma and Ted strolled arm in arm behind us. "With me *and* Grandma?"

"Might as well make it coffee for four." He unlocked the door to my cottage and waved us all inside ahead of me.

I froze. Across the wall behind my dinette table was painted in red the words 'I'm coming'. "I guess that means none of the poker guys are the culprit."

"Ida, give me your gun." Ted held out his hand for her pink Glock. "The three of you step outside while I check the rest of the place. Someone call Seth."

"Go with him, Heath. He can't go alone." Grandma clutched her Tazor. "I'll guard Shelby. I really wish you'd start carrying the weapons I got you. Seriously. It's almost as if you want to die."

I rolled my eyes. "Go ahead Heath. We'll be fine out here."

He hesitated before nodding and following Ted.

I pulled my cell phone from my pocket and called Seth. "Someone left me a message in my cottage."

He groaned. "I'm on my way. Just one night of sleep without dealing with you would be a true blessing." Click.

Ted and Heath told us we could come in just as Seth was racing down the walkway.

"We didn't find anything other than the message," Heath said. "Only you can really tell if anything is missing, though."

"I'm sure the message was the whole point. I've nothing anyone wants." I lived a simple life with second-hand clothes, a furnished cottage, and food prepared by a chef. Nothing of value for anyone to steal except my life.

"Let me look before you touch anything." Seth rushed inside only to join us moments later agreeing with the other two men. "Yep. Just the message." He snapped a photo of it with his phone. "Red paint."

"I'll be back with something to cover it with." Heath jogged out the front door.

I plopped on the sofa and removed my coat while staring at the dripping message on my white wall. It might be paint, but the way it ran down the wall resembled blood. I shuddered. "Ted, I'd like a security camera installed, please. One I can access from my phone."

He nodded. "You'll have it in the morning."

~

I had a lot of things in the morning, including two cameras Ted had covering every door and window of my cottage. In addition, I had a full marching band of a headache, a grumpy grandmother in the shower in an attempt to wash away the night's lack of sleep, and an overly excited mother.

"This time I agree with your grandmother. Start carrying your gun." She stared at the freshly painted wall Heath had done last night.

"Okay. Any news on the residents?" I sat on the sofa, feet on the coffee table, and a cup of coffee in my hand.

"Nope. But that just means any news is hidden." She sat across from me. "I've been careful not to say a word to anyone, but everyone seems to know I'm looking for something."

I stiffened. "What do you mean?"

"That Rita Hayworth look-a-like, Mrs. Lorriane Hardy didn't take kindly to me asking for family references. Seems her blood is too blue to be questioned. Then, Scott dashed off right away when he spotted some information on my printer—"

"What kinds of things?"

"Any details and news articles I could find on your previous snooping episodes." She blew in her mug of coffee. "Then, Alice said to stop using my work time to snoop, Joyce threw a cookie across the room when she spotted an article on that crazy Susan woman. The whole place has gone nuts."

"Stop investigating, Mom. Spread the word that you've given up." I couldn't live if something happened to her because of me.

"Nonsense. I think I'm developing a knack for this sort of thing, as much as I hate to say so."

"It's too dangerous."

"Yes, it is." She gave me a sharp look. "I don't see you stopping."

"Someone is trying to kill me!"

She shrugged. "So it seems. I'll see you at breakfast in exactly fifteen minutes. Heath will be here to pick you up."

"No need. I'm awake." A fully dressed, made-up Grandma bounced from the bathroom. "Good as new after a shower. I'm the official bodyguard. No need for Heath."

"Maybe I just like having him around," I said, setting my half-empty mug on the table.

"That's different." She grinned and tossed me a jacket. "Are you wearing those sweats? Didn't you sleep in them?"

"Yes, and yes." I donned my coat and glared. "I'm a gardener, not a fashion plate."

"No reason you can't dig in the dirt and still look nice." She pulled her gun and yanked open the front door as someone knocked. "A woman needs to look nice at all times if she wants to keep her man."

"Nice, Ida." Heath glowered. "You almost shot me."

"Not even close." She glanced around outside. "All clear."

If it wouldn't mean jail time for assaulting a police officer, I'd hit Seth the next time I saw him. Giving Grandma this much power had to be the worst idea ever.

She led the way to breakfast with the rest of us

following. Any noise had her pointing her gun in that direction. Someone really would wind up hurt...or dead. I would have to talk to Ted. Maybe he could rein her in.

I spotted him the moment we entered the hall. "You have to do something." I pointed to where Grandma rested her weapon on the table. "She's waving that thing around like she's Dirty Harriet."

"I'll have Seth take it away from her. She can make do with her Tazor. Less lethal."

"Thank you." Relief flooded through me with tsunami force. I planted a quick kiss on his weathered cheek and headed for the buffet.

Soon, I was at my usual table loaded down with biscuits, gravy, and bacon. I refused to let the alarming message from the night before interfere with my appetite. A girl couldn't work if she were starving. Right?

"Danger doesn't seem to be bothering you too much." Scott sat next to me.

"Don't let April see you. She'll kick you out." She didn't allow anyone but staff and residents to enter the dining hall.

"She's locked in her office, again." He plucked at a napkin. "I need to speak to you with a concern regarding your mother."

"Okay." I set down my fork and gave him my full attention. "Shoot."

"She shouldn't be investigating who is threatening you. She's a sweet, middle-aged woman who is in way over her head."

"I agree. If you know of a way to stop her, I'm all ears."

"I really like her. I don't want anything to happen to her."

"Neither do I."

He sighed, tearing the napkin into small pieces that formed a tiny white paper mountain. "I'll think of something." He stood and hurried from the room.

It wasn't until he'd left that I realized that while he spoke to me, he hadn't made eye contact once. Yes, Scott had always been on the shy side, but I thought we were past all that and were friends after I caught the murderer of his girlfriend. Maybe he was more worried than he wanted to say.

I glanced toward the door he'd exited from. We did agree on one thing. Mom needed to stay out of my problems.

5

"*H*arvey Weston was killed in prison last Friday." Grandma plopped onto the sofa next to me the next morning.

"What? How do you know?" I straightened from my comfy slouch.

"I eavesdropped on Seth telling Ted. For a cop, that young man has loose lips." She grinned. "You should find out who had the connection to him. Then we find the person trying to kill you."

"Don't be too hard on Seth. He's only relying on Ted's experience." I grabbed my laptop and typed in Weston's name. The newspaper article about his arrest, then one about his death came up first. "Wow. Shanked in the shower with a sharpened toothbrush. The guards think it might be gang related."

"I've always thought your father's death might have been." Grandma studied her nails. "Something about it didn't make sense. Your father was too smart to get caught unawares during a routine traffic stop."

My heart skipped a beat. Could Dad's death have been gang related? He'd been a cop after all, and done some undercover work when he was a younger detective. I finished reading the articles and did some more searching. "I need to get into Ted's computer. Is it password protected?"

"Yes, but I'm sure I can figure it out. What do you need there?" She peered over my shoulder.

"The records on Harvey that I can't get to on my own." I closed my laptop and scrunched my mouth in thought. If we were dealing with someone connected to the mob, why me? I'd never had any affiliation. Never met a member that I knew of. "Let's talk to Mom." Maybe she knew some things from Dad's past she'd never spoken about.

Mom was already behind her desk, furiously typing on her desktop computer. "I'm busy," she said, not looking up. "Alice has something that must go out."

"It's important, Mom. It's about Dad."

She stopped typing, removed her glasses, and stared up at us. "Why?"

I explained about Harvey being killed and his gang affiliation. "Did Dad have anything to do with gangs when he was a detective?"

"That was before you were born. He stepped down after that because of the danger, not wanting to leave you without a father." Tears welled in her eyes. "It didn't work though, did it?"

"No." My throat clogged. "You haven't answered my question."

She heaved a heavy sigh. "Yes, he had a lot of run

ins with the gangs during that time. Maybe even when he stepped down and no longer did undercover work. He spoke less and less about his work toward the end. I often suspected he might be in danger."

"Why?" I leaned over the counter, my gaze glued to hers.

"He checked and double checked all doors and windows before we went to bed at night, installed a security system, and was emphatic I make sure it was turned on when he left the house and any time you and I were home alone." She grabbed a Kleenex from a desk drawer and blew her nose. "He would be devastated to think his career brought danger to you."

"We don't know that it has." Although I strongly suspected it had.

"Come with me." She set the phone to forward calls to her cell phone. "I have something for you. I think now is the right time."

After putting a 'Back Soon' sign on her desk, she led us to her apartment where she pulled a locked metal box slightly larger than a box boots might come in from the top shelf of her closet. She handed me a folded piece of paper. "Here's the combination. I don't know if this box holds what you're looking for, but it might be a start. I've never opened it."

"Why didn't you give this to Seth?" The box was heavy in my arms. "If you think this might be related to the greenhouse incident, he would want to have it."

"He didn't ask." She gave a wry smile. "Now go see if you can stop someone from killing you. Maybe you can even find justice for your father while you're at it."

I sincerely hoped so. Nothing would give me

greater pleasure.

I carried the box to my cottage and hid it in the hamper under a load of clothes waiting to be laundered. Silly, maybe, but I wasn't taking any chances of this box disappearing, and who wanted to dig through dirty clothes to find something important?

"Aren't you going to open it?" Grandma leaned against the door jamb.

"Tonight."

"When you're alone, you mean." She looked hurt.

"Yes. No, offense, but the contents might be personal. If there's anything pertaining to someone trying to kill me, I'll let you see."

"I suppose." She gave a sly grin. "Ted is meeting some of his bodies at the Elk's Lodge tonight. We can try to get into his computer."

That would mean delaying opening the metal box, but it might be our only chance to snoop without getting caught. "Deal. Call me the minute he leaves."

I locked my cottage and headed back to the main building where I'd left my golf cart. Grandma had said she'd try to get hints as to Ted's password. I could only hope she didn't blow our plan.

After peeking in to see Mom furiously typing away again, I drove the cart around the grounds before heading for the greenhouse. I parked and traipsed completely around the building to make sure nothing out of the ordinary was waiting for me. When everything seemed fine, I turned the door handle and nudged the door open with my foot. So far so good. I wasn't sure what I expected, or even if anyone would try killing me in the same way or not, but I wasn't taking any chances.

By the time the lunch bell rang, I was happily still alive and not foggy minded in the least. I practically had a skip in my step as I headed to lunch. Until I saw the scowl on Alice's face, which happened to be trained on me before I could step inside the building.

"Did I forget to do something?" I grinned.

"Your grandmother is a menace." She crossed her arms.

Uh-oh. "What has she done now?"

"She is standing right inside that door..."she pointed to the entrance, "...interrogating everyone who steps inside. She said it's her job as your bodyguard to keep out suspicious people."

"I'll talk to her." I shoved inside. "Grandma, a word, please."

"I'm working." She narrowed her eyes at one of our elderly residents.

"Stop it. You're not here to bother people, just watch my back."

"That's what I'm doing."

"No, you're harassing people." I took her by the arm and led her to our normal table. "Heath, I need you to babysit her while I get my lunch." I fixed a stern look on Grandma. "You can get your food when I return."

"I'll escort her," Heath said.

That's one of the things I love about the man. He'll do what I ask without question. Most of the time. Or he'll at least wait until we're alone before he questions me.

I grabbed a chicken salad sandwich and a bowl of soup while Grandma did her best to coerce Heath into leaving her to her own devices. I smiled and headed for the table.

My cell phone buzzed in my pocket. Once I sat down, I checked and saw a text message from my best friend Cheryl. Then more immediately dinged through.

What do you mean someone tried to kill you?

Why did I have to hear this from Seth?

Why didn't you call me?

Uh-oh. I had some explaining today.

I typed back that I would call her later.

"What's wrong?" Heath pulled a chair out for Grandma, then sat next to me.

"I never called Cheryl about being poisoned. Her text sounds mad."

"Once you apologize and explain how crazy things have been, she'll forgive you." Heath put his hand over mine.

"I hope so. I'm going to take my lunch home and give her a call before starting work again." I gave him a kiss on his cheek, told Grandma to stay and eat before following me, and set my lunch on a tray to carry home.

Once there, I set the tray on the coffee table and called Cheryl. "I'm sorry."

"You should be." She sighed. "I only have fifteen minutes before I pick up my class from lunch. Talk fast."

I gave her the nutshell version of almost dying and what I'd been busy with since. When I'd finished, I exhaled slowly. "That's it."

She sighed. "I miss out on everything by not working there."

"No students to be taught here at Shady Acres."

"You got out."

"I couldn't stay after being jilted at the altar. You know that."

"Spring break is so far away." She groaned dramatically. "I'll come up next weekend and participate a bit. Maybe I'll call in sick on Monday."

She always spent the holidays with me if I was involved in a mystery. Coming close to death a few times didn't seem to deter my five-foot-eleven-inch, buxom, Amazon friend.

"That sounds like a great idea. You can help get Grandma off my back."

"That sounds like fun. See you Friday!" Click.

Friendship saved, I stared down the hall while I ate my lunch, really wanting to open the locked box. But, if I did, and it was something horrible, I'd never get any more work done. Same if it was something wonderful. Better to do it last thing of the day so I could have time to process what I found.

When I'd finished eating, I carried the tray back to the dining hall and went to dig up the few poinsettia's leftover from Christmas that had decided to bite the dust. I knelt and spread mulch over the bare ground. Replanting would have to wait until spring. I started to straighten.

A hand shoved in the middle of my back, sending me face first into the mulch. What felt like a booted foot held me there. Dirt filled my mouth and nostrils. After several seconds, I started to panic and grabbed fistfuls of the dirt, tossing them randomly behind me. My attacker never spoke a word, just held me in place. The attacker wanted me to suffocate!

I moved my face back and forth until I'd cleared a small pocket of air. The booted foot pressed harder. If only I had a garden tool in my hand. The person wouldn't like having it sticking in their leg very well.

Spots were starting to appear before my eyes. I could breath, but barely, and fear was grabbing a tight hold of my emotions. I grappled with my hands behind me. I came into contact with what felt like a steel-toed boot. I screamed through the mouthful of dirt. What emerged from my throat was more of a shriek.

A hand now pressed the back of my head. Where was Grandma? This one time she wasn't as close as my shadow and I was attacked. If I didn't die, I'd never push her away again.

"You've a debt to pay." A hoarse whisper next to my ear sent my skin crawling. "His death is on your hands."

What death? What debt?

A bash to the head and my world went dark.

6

"Shelby!"

I woke to Grandma shaking me. My head pounded. A quick feel of the back of my skull presented a bump.

"Come on. We need a doctor to take a look at your head." She pulled out her cellphone. Minutes later, Heath came running.

"What happened?" He gathered me in his arms and headed for my cottage.

"Grandma wants me to go to the doctor, but it's just a bump on the head." I closed my eyes and leaned my head against his strong chest.

"Good for you that Harold Ball's nephew, who happens to be a doctor, is visiting. Ida, could you go fetch him?"

Grandma must have nodded, because I heard the click of her heels moving away at a fast pace.

Heath carried me to the sofa in my cottage and

placed a pillow under my head. "Don't go to sleep." He perched on the coffee table. "Tell me what happened?"

I did, watching his face darken with each word from my mouth. "I must look a fright with dirt on my face and shoved up my nose."

"You're beautiful, and more importantly, alive." He brushed my hair back from my face. "I'm calling Seth. Then, I'll get you something to wash your face with."

Someone was always having to call Seth. I sighed and draped my arm across my eyes not opening them until Grandma, Ted, Seth, and a man I didn't know but who carried the infamous black bag of a doctor, entered my living room. That was another question I had. Why did any trouble I get myself into warrant an entire crowd of people to witness my misfortune?

The doctor, also named Harold Ball after his uncle, examined my head and shined a penlight into my eyes. "A mild concussion. You'll be fine. I'll write you a prescription for pain meds."

"I still have some from the last time."

"The way you get hurt, take the prescription," Grandma said.

"Fine." I took the paper. "How long am I down for?"

"Just today. You might have a headache tomorrow, but you don't need to stay bedridden." He smiled and left, leaving the spot next to me open for a scowling Seth.

"I thought I had it worked out for someone to be with you at all times?" He glared at Grandma.

"Don't look at me. She took off before I was finished eating." Grandma held up her hands.

"Ida…" he growled.

"Fine. But I don't see how a little old lady will deter a killer." She plopped on the opposite end of the sofa. "Especially since Teddy took my gun away."

I raised wide eyes to Seth. "Can't you find someone else?"

"Everyone else has a job. She's the only one available." He motioned for Heath to move from the coffee table, then took his place. "Tell me everything that happened."

So, I said it all again. "That's it."

"Are you sure you didn't get a look at the guy?"

"The only thing I know for sure is that it was a man and he wore steel-toed boots." I glanced at Heath's feet. "Probably like the ones Heath wears. A ton of men wear them."

"Okay. You know what to do if you remember anything." He pressed his lips together, stood and stared down at me. "Try to stay out of trouble."

"I'm doing my best. Trouble seems to follow me like a deer to a salt brick." I glanced around him to see Grandma pointing to her phone. Oh. Ted must be gone. "Everyone out. I need to rest. I'm suddenly very tired."

Seth and Heath stared at me as if I'd grown a third eye.

"What are you up to?" Seth asked.

"What do you mean?" I tried to look confused, which probably didn't take much doing. I was pretty sure I looked that way most of the time.

"We aren't up to anything." Grandma made shooing motions with her hands. "We aren't leaving the cottage. No worries."

I smiled, although I wondered how we would

snoop through Ted's laptop without leaving. "See? I'll be fine."

"Hmm." Heath gave me a kiss. "We'll see. I'll call you in a bit to check on you."

"Okay." I took his hand, letting my fingers slip through his as he went.

He stopped and studied my face for a minute. "Are you all right?"

"Just wondering which time will be the last time I set eyes on you."

He leaned down for another kiss. One that left me woozier than the knock on the head.

"That won't happen. Not this time. I love you." He caressed my cheek, and then left.

"I love you," I whispered after him.

"Okay, enough mooshiness." Grandma pulled her big yellow bag from behind the sofa. "I filched this before I came over. We only have an hour before Teddy is back. I thought those men would never leave."

Despite the twenty-five miners with pickaxes in my head, I sat up and placed Ted's laptop on my lap. "What's the password?"

"I don't know."

I glanced at her. "I thought you said you were going to get it out of him."

"I tried." She tapped a manicured nail against her teeth. "Try my name."

"Not long enough."

"Oh." She grinned. "Try sugar lips. All one word. That's what Teddy calls me when we're alone."

I typed in the word. "Bingo." As I browsed his search history, a lot of information on Harvey Weston came up…along with the information that not only had

Harvey gone into Witness Protection, but he had a son. Because the son had been a minor at the time, his name was left out of the report. I'd need to dig deeper to find out his identity. Deeper than Ted had access to.

Still, I'd bet my Volkswagon that Harvey's son was the one behind the attacks on me. "You need to return this immediately."

"That would mean leaving you alone." She shook her head.

"Just hurry. I'll make sure the doors and windows are locked. You have your key, right?"

"Yes." She dug her Tazer from her purse. "I'll be right back."

I knew it would take her ten minutes to make the return trip. Not enough time for me to dig into Dad's locked box. But, I could run a hot bath and use it as a pretense to dig through his things. The bathroom was the one room where Grandma left me alone.

My cell phone rang. It was Heath.

"Why has Ida left you alone?"

"Where are you?" I got up and peered through a slit in the curtains.

"Across from your cottage keeping an eye on you."

"Honey, it's too cold for that. I'm fine. The door is locked." Oh, I loved that man.

"It is chilly. I'll go home when Ida returns. How's the head?"

"Did you know that Harvey Weston had a son, also in Witness Protection? And did you also know that the son was put in a different location?"

"How did you find this out?"

I sat on the arm of the chair. "Don't get mad, but Grandma and I snooped through Ted's laptop."

"That's why you wanted us out."

"Well, Seth mostly."

"Here comes Ida. Good night, Shelby."

"Good night." I hung up and opened the door for my bodyguard.

"Coast is clear. Not a soul out except for The Vampire. He promised to keep an eye on your place."

Good old Lawrence. "Great. I'm going to take a hot bath."

"I'll make some chamomile tea for when you're out. You'll sleep like a baby." She went to the kitchen while I hurried to the bathroom. After locking the door, I dug the box out of the hamper and turned on the water. I'd have to take a real bath eventually, Grandma would notice my deception right off if I didn't, but first things first.

With shaking hands, I unlocked the box. I said a quick prayer and slowly lifted the lid. Inside rested several files. I took a deep breath and lifted the first one.

"Carmen Sanchez." Further reading showed he was the leader of a gang centered in Boonesville. I didn't even know our town had a gang. We never had a problem with graffiti. Maybe they caused all their trouble in the larger city of Warner.

The more I read, the more I was convinced Dad had died at the hands of the Yellow Jackets. Tears pricked my eyes.

A knock at the door startled me, causing the files to slide to the floor. "That tub must be overflowing by now," Grandma shouted. "If you don't answer, I'm coming in."

"I'm fine." A sob choked off my words.

Grandma knocked on the door. "What are you doing? Why are you crying? What's in the box?"

I heard something grate in the lock.

Grandma, holding one of those little door opener thingings, entered. She reached over and turned off the water before gathering the files back together.

"A gang did kill Dad. I'm certain of it. Now, I need to learn all I can about the Yellow Jackets. I think they may be targeting me now."

"Why? You're nothing more than the gardener of a retirement community. No threat at all to them." She sat on the edge of the tub. "Would you like me to draw you a real bath?"

"In a minute." I needed to think about what to do. I supposed the next people to talk to would be Seth and Ted. They would be the best at keeping me safe and getting to the bottom of all this. "I need to go to the precinct tomorrow and talk to Seth."

"I'll drive you. No sense taking chances with your concussion. We'll take the van."

I groaned. I hated the ancient thing with all its creaks, groans, and rust spots, but Grandma loved it. She kept promising a new paint job to go with the new engine, but so far that hadn't happened. "Can't you drive my car?"

"Nope. I like sitting up high. Makes me feel like a queen." She turned on the hot water and poured in a liberal amount of lavender bath bubbles while I placed the box back in the hamper. "You'll sleep like a baby when I'm finished taking care of you."

Speaking of… "Where's Mom?"

"Out on a date. She has no idea you've been attacked…again. I figured we could let her know tomorrow. That girl needs to get out more and not have her daughter chill her vibe."

For crying out loud. "She's going to be furious that no one told her."

"She'll get over it. Now, strip and get in that water. I'll be back with your tea." She glanced at the window over the tub. "You really should hang a curtain there. If someone stood on a milk crate, they could see in. You never know when a Peeping Tom will wander by." She left me nervous now about someone watching me bathe.

I stood and lined up the shampoo, conditioner, and bubble bath bottles, then tossed a washrag over them. It didn't cover the whole window, but did a fairly good job. Just as I started to turn, I caught a glimpse of someone watching from the woods behind my cottage.

The figure wasn't tall and thin enough to be Leroy. "Grandma!"

She rushed into the bathroom, sliding to a halt. "What in heaven's name are you doing staring out the window as naked as the day you were born?"

"There is someone outside." I grabbed a towel and wrapped it around me. I'd be embarrassed about my nudity later. "Call Ted."

"And put my teddy bear in danger? No way." She stepped into the tub with me, pulling her cell phone from her pocket. She slid the window open and snapped a photo.

Whoever it was in the shadows turned and ran. "Call Seth. He can at least see if there are any prints." I stepped out of the water and hurried to get dressed.

"What about your bath?"

"I'm finished." I grabbed a pair of sweat pants and

sweat shirt, slid my feet into thick wool-lined slippers and grabbed the gun Grandma had given me for Christmas. The one I had to shoot. Then, clutching the gun, I yanked open the back door and raced into the woods, Grandma right behind me.

I needed some answers and this person had them.

7

*M*y head throbbed with every pound of my footsteps. Still, I raced on, determined to confront my attacker. I was armed, and I was angry.

Inside the forest was dark. Like dead of night dark. Even with the skeletal branches of trees in January, the cloudy night blocked off the moonlight.

Grandma grasped my shoulders. "Seriously? I'm too old to be running off half-cocked."

"You could have stayed behind."

"Nope. I'm your bodyguard." She planted her hands on her knees and panted. "Just so you know...Heath is going to be very upset at your foolishness."

"Foolishness?" I hissed. "This might very well be the man that killed my father."

"And could very well be the one that succeeds in killing you." She straightened and planted her fists on her hips, for once the voice of reason. "I'm just saying not to run in there blinded by fury."

"You're right." I trudged ahead slower and quieter. Not that it likely mattered. I'm sure the culprit was long gone. Still, we might pick up his tracks somewhere.

A light glowed. I whirled. "Turn that phone off."

"I'm texting Teddy and Heath to let them know where we are. I have them on a group text with Seth." Her teeth flashed. "Smart, huh? There. Sent and on vibrate."

I shook my head and proceeded, widening my eyes in hopes of seeing better. It didn't work. The man watching my cottage could be standing three feet from me, shielded by a tree trunk, and I'd never see him. "It's useless. We might as well head back."

Of course we ran into a frantic Ted and Heath on our way.

"Of all the hare-brained, stupid, irresponsible—" Ted sputtered, then stopped and sighed. "It's no use. You don't have the sense God gave a goose sometimes."

"You must be speaking to Shelby," Grandma said, patting his cheek. "I know you wouldn't speak to your fiancé that way."

Heath didn't say anything, just fell into step beside me, his gaze darting into the shadows. I wasn't fooled. He'd have a ton of questions once we returned to my place.

We trooped through the door I'd left open in my rush outside and plopped onto the sofa. I glanced at the men's faces when they returned from checking out the other rooms for predators. "I'll explain everything when Seth gets here." I picked at a hole in my sweatpants. I'd have to come clean about my suspicions regarding Dad's death, the box of files…everything. I glanced at Grandma.

From the wide-eyed look on her face, she knew she was in trouble once Ted found out about her taking his laptop. I sighed. What a mess.

"Coffee?" Grandma, face pale, glanced around the room.

"Might as well," Ted said. "I have a feeling we'll be here awhile."

"Is this an intervention?" she asked.

"Close to it."

My startled gaze met Heath's. An intervention for what? Wanting justice for my father? Surely not.

Seth stood in the doorway and glared. "Not the smartest thing to do, Shelby."

I shrugged. "I have my reasons." I motioned for him to sit. "Chasing someone who might be a killer may not be the wisest thing I've ever done, but I strongly believe my father's death is connected to what's happening with me."

From Seth's stony look, this wasn't a surprise to him. "You knew?" I couldn't believe he'd withheld information from me.

"Suspected." He cocked his head. "How did you come to this conclusion?"

I explained about the box, about finding out Harvey was most likely killed by a gang, and skirted around the whole witness protection thing. "I'm thinking Harvey may have family somewhere. Family that blames me for his death. Isn't that silly? I don't know anyone in prison."

All three men narrowed their eyes at me. Heath out

of anger and pain that I kept information from him, the others because they suspected I came about some of my information a bit unethically. At least that's what I thought they were thinking. Not being a mind reader, I had to go with facial expressions. And their's were shouting.

"I suspect," Ted said, accepting a mug of coffee from Grandma, "that these two delinquents broke into my laptop and found out about the family." His gaze speared mine. "I also suspect that you, Seth, should take a look at what is in Mr. Hart's box."

"I'll get it." I stood.

"No, you can tell me where it is." Seth held out his arm to prevent me from getting away. "I don't want anything hidden."

"It's hidden under my dirty underwear. Still want to fetch it?" I tilted my chin.

He shuddered. "Heath, go with her."

I didn't want him to see my unmentionables either, but he was better than marble-faced Seth. I led the way down the hall and to the restroom. After retrieving the box, I took a deep breath and faced Heath. "I'm sorry. Everything is happening so fast I didn't take the time to fill you in."

"Do you realize how much that hurts me?" He leaned against the door jamb. "I've been lenient in letting you solve the mysteries, offering my help, and now you're keeping me out of the loop and putting not only yourself, but Ida in danger." He ran his fingers through his hair, causing the strands to stand on end. "I'm not sure if I can deal with that."

"What does that mean? Are you breaking up with me?"

Pain clouded his eyes. "I don't know." He stepped back and waved me ahead of him. "I love you, Shelby, but I don't know how much more I can take. You can't keep things from me. You either trust me or you don't. This thing about your father...I'd like to help you."

I nodded. "I'll do better. I promise." I spotted Seth watching from the end of the hall. "Don't worry. We just needed to talk a little." I handed him the box and resumed my seat on the sofa.

"We aren't finished talking," Heath whispered before taking his seat.

I groaned inwardly. "Now what?"

Seth remained standing. "I'll take this box to the precinct and study the files. I'll make sure you get them back when this case is solved."

"It's been five years and my father's death is unsolved." I crossed my arms. "I don't have much hope you'll solve it."

"Look, Shelby." His jaw hardened. "There are things at work you know nothing about. Stop risking your life and the lives of those around you and let me do my job." He stormed from the cottage.

"He's right," Ted said. "Even if Seth weren't involved, I thought we were all a team. Teams share information and keep each other safe. Not steal laptops and break passwords." He gave Grandma a peck on the cheek and followed Seth.

Heath headed for my linen closet, grabbed a pillow and a blanket and stared down at me. "You're sitting on my bed."

~

Heath waited at the kitchen table the next morning, a cup of coffee and a newspaper in front of him. I smiled, thoroughly enjoying a view I could have for the rest of my life if I would only set a wedding date and learn to let him know where I was going when the situation warranted. Not that Heath was overbearing, only caring. I shouldn't mind keeping him informed.

After his declaration last night that he would now be staying in the cottage with Grandma and me, I'd tossed and turned over the trouble I'd caused. Still, I had no intention of backing down. I would find justice for my father. If Heath wanted to help, I'd gladly let him. As long as he didn't stifle me.

"Good morning," I said softly, trying to gauge his mood.

"I hope so." He didn't look up.

Alrighty then. He was still upset. "Are you ready for breakfast? Where's Grandma?"

"Ted already picked her up. Yes, I'm ready." He folded his paper, set his mug in the sink, and ushered me out the door. "The only way I can think of for both of us to get our work done if for us to take turns. What's on your list for today?"

"I have a light day. Nothing more than planning this weekend's social event. I can do that anywhere." It would most likely be Bingo since I'd been a little pre-occupied.

"Good. I have some repairs in a couple of the cottages."

"How long will you be angry with me?" I peered up from lowered lashes.

"Until I know you trust me."

"I do!"

"Then you'll have to prove it." He held open the dining room door.

I felt as if there was a clock ticking and time was running out on Heath's patience. Fear welled in me, choking off my words. I wanted to tell him how sorry I was, how much I loved him, but what if I did and I failed to earn back his trust? Could we survive that? In all honesty, I couldn't say I wouldn't mess up again.

He turned and held out his hand. "Come on."

I slipped mine in his, feeling safer than I had in days. I gave a shy smile. He smiled back and leaned in for a kiss. "We'll be fine, Shelby."

Tears pricked my eyes. All I could do was nod.

He situated me at our usual table and went to fill our plates for breakfast.

While he was gone, I rested my elbows on the table and stared at my mother who gave me a look that should have turned me to ash. "What?"

"I heard what happened while I was on my date with Bob. Would a text have been so hard?"

"It would have ruined your evening." Darn Grandma and her big mouth. "I was going to tell you today."

"And, Heath is staying at your cottage? That's not very proper."

"Grandma is a more than sufficient chaperone."

"Pshaw." She shook her head. "That's like saying a two-year-old is a chaperone."

"Would it make you feel better to know Cheryl is coming for a few days on Friday?"

"A bit. She's always been a good girl."

I pressed my lips together to keep quiet. What Mom didn't know wouldn't hurt her. "I'm sorry, Mom. I've been apologizing to a lot of people lately."

"If you'd only lean on others, you wouldn't have

to." She breathed deeply through her nose. "Now that we've gotten that out of the way, it's off to work for me." She flashed a grin and left.

I lowered my arms and let my head fall forward. I was batting a thousand in the 'doing wrong' department.

"Get up, get up, get up." Grandma yanked my arm from under my head. "Seth is searching the woods for clues. If we hurry, we can help him."

"I feel like we should stay out of his way for a day or two."

"There's no fun in that!" She glowered. "Let's go."

"I have to let Heath know."

"I already did. He's making you a breakfast burrito so you can carry it with you." She grinned, clearly pleased with herself.

Heath waited at the door. He handed me my burrito and opened the door for us to go ahead of him. "You know we can't interfere, right?"

"Of course," Grandma and I said in unison.

He groaned.

By the time we arrived, Seth had strung crime scene tape around the area. "Stay back. I mean it."

"Can we watch?" That way, we'd at least see if he discovered anything.

"Just stay out of the way."

Somebody was in a bad mood. I shrugged at Grandma and took a bite of my burrito. Jalapenos! I glanced up at Heath.

"Oops. I gave you mine." He switched with me, barely holding back his laughter.

If I was to bet, I'd say he did it on purpose as a tiny payment toward me leaving him out of the loop. "Not funny."

We watched as crime scene techs moved past us.

"Gee," Grandma said. "I had no idea last night would result in this much excitement."

Seth approached the other side of the tape. "Heath, what size shoe do you wear?"

"Eleven, why?"

"I need your foot for comparison."

8

*O*nce Seth confirmed that the set of prints on the path didn't belong to one of us, he said with certainty that the perp wore a size eleven shoe. Wonderful. That sounded like a common size to me.

I followed Heath to cottage thirty one and sat at the kitchen table while he fixed a leaky kitchen sink. "Who lives here?"

"Someone just moved out," he said, his head under the sink. "Someone new coming tomorrow."

Sometimes Shady Acres was a revolving door. What I never could understand was why someone would move out of such a beautiful place. Sure, a few tenants had died, most of which I'd gotten involved with their deaths one way or the other. But, to willingly leave…I shrugged.

Of course, when Heath and I married, and babies came along, we'd have to go. Hopefully, back to the house I grew up in. Cheryl rented it for the time being, but she'd understand.

Silly how the directions the mind went when idle. I drummed my fingers on the tabletop. How could I find out who Harvey Weston's son is? I doubted the information would be easy to find even for Seth. Since the son had been a minor at the time of relocation, the FBI would have sealed his records tighter than a turtle closing into his shell.

"What are you cooking up now?" Heath had stood and now wiped his hands on a rag.

"Just wondering how we can find out who Harvey's son is."

"We don't even know whether the boy is still alive."

"He'd be a man now. You're right. I shouldn't waste time on something I'll never have access to." If the son was the one trying to kill me, we'd meet eventually. I always came face-to-face with the killer at some point. Lucky me. "So, what do I do in the meantime?"

"Do you really think your father was killed by the Yellow Jackets?"

"I think so."

"Then let's concentrate on that."

"How?"

"Tonight, we'll find out everything we can about them online. Then, we hit the streets."

My mouth dried up. "Asking questions about an active gang is probably the most dangerous thing we'll have ever done."

"It's all I can think of right now. Maybe you can get a list of the officers your father worked with. They could fill in some of the blanks and tell us the best way to proceed."

I grinned. "Have I ever told you that you're a genius?"

He returned the grin. "Nope."

"Well, you are." I moved closer and wrapped my arms around his waist, gazing into his face. "Partners?"

"Absolutely."

His next job was changing the locks in the suite of Lorraine Hardy. Seems the woman is convinced someone has been sneaking into her apartment when she isn't home.

While Heath did that, I moved to her window. The third floor suite in the main building had a great view of the grounds. A person could see almost every corner of Shady Acres. The woman scored with this place.

"It's a great view, isn't it?" Lorraine strolled from the bedroom wearing a silk lounge set and looking as if she'd stepped out of 1942. She even held a skinny cigarette in a cream-colored filter. "Unfortunately, I don't feel safe."

"How often do you leave your apartment?" I let the curtains fall into place.

"Every day, except for today and Saturdays. I do voice overs on commercials."

I could see that. Her soft, sultry voice was perfect for radio and television. "You'll be fine with the locks changed."

"I sincerely hope so. A single gal can't be too careful." She relaxed on a chaise lounge and blew a smoke ring over her head.

The main building apartments didn't come furnished and Lorraine had done hers 1940s vintage. If

I didn't have a cellphone in my pocket, I'd think I'd traveled back in time.

"There you go." Heath handed her a new set of keys. "Peace of mind."

"Sweetheart, if only I were twenty years younger."

I rolled my eyes. More like thirty years if I wanted to get particular.

Heath chuckled. "Call if you need something else."

"Oh, sweetheart, I won't hesitate."

"Wow," I said, as soon as we stepped into the hall. "You even set the hearts of sixty year old women aflutter."

"It's a gift." He tossed me a wink. "But I only want a certain twenty-eight-year-old." He snaked his arm around my waist and pulled me close for a quick kiss. Once my knees were weak, he pulled back. "Let's go see if your mother has a list of retired officers."

"Huh?" I blinked.

"Men who once worked with your father."

"Oh, yeah." I took a deep breath. Focus, Shelby. "Then lunch."

"You eat a lot for such a tiny thing." He pressed the button on the elevator.

Once the doors slid shut, he pressed the button for the lobby. The car dropped a foot and stopped.

Heath pressed the button again. "What the heck?"

I couldn't help but remember the time we'd been in the elevator and the building caught fire. I pushed against the door. "We have to get out."

"Settle down. Let me think." He pressed the red help button.

"We don't have the staff to come rescue us." I stared up at him. "Where does that button even go?"

"Alice's office."

"Great. She'll know just what to do." I continued trying to pry the doors open.

What if my would-be killer planned this? I sniffed. What if gas was seeping into the elevator at that very minute? I pulled my tee-shirt over my nose. Or…what if when the doors did open, someone stood on the other side and sprayed us with bullets?

My breathing quickened. Which definitely didn't bode well if gas was blowing in.

"Shelby, look at me." Heath turned me to face him. "Relax." He pulled my shirt back into place.

I glanced over our head. "Why aren't there any escape panels?"

"That's only in the movies."

"Oh, God, help us." I really was praying this time. Yes, I knew that those times were rare, but I was getting desperate.

"Let me think." Heath gave me a look that clearly told me to be still and quiet.

As time passed and the elevator didn't move, nor did the doors open or anyone come to our rescue, Heath started fluttering his fingers against his thigh. A sure sign of growing nervousness.

"Why isn't something happening?" I asked. "If someone wanted to harm us, they wouldn't just lock us in an elevator. Someone is bound to come along at some point."

"They'll take the stairs if the elevator doesn't work."

"Right." So much for making myself feel better. I slid to the floor, my back against the side wall. I pulled out my cell phone. "Come on. I need a miracle here."

One bar fluttered to life. Usually, I couldn't get service in the elevator shaft. I punched in Ted's number.

"Heath and I are stuck in the elevator!" I said the words as fast as possible, wanting to get out our need for help before service disappeared.

I stared at a blank screen. Too late. "I don't think the call went through."

"We wait." He sat next to me. "What has me stumped is why? Why lock us in the elevator just to wait? If someone wanted to harm us, we're at their mercy."

"You aren't helping my nerves."

"I'm convinced it's a coincidence."

"You don't think we're in danger?"

"No." He put his arm around my shoulders and let me rest against him. "Someone will come along."

And they did. After three hours, Ted and an elevator repair man pried open the doors.

"You got my message?"

"Yep, but I was down south taking care of personal business," Ted said. "Took me a while to get here and the elevator service company was booked solid. Sorry about that." He held down a hand and helped me up to the third floor. "I've been here for about half an hour before this guy showed."

"Sorry." The overweight man set to work the moment Heath climbed out. "Huh."

"What?" I asked as the rest of us crowded around him.

"There's a pipe wedged in the mechanism. Someone trapped y'all on purpose."

I glanced up at Heath. "See?"

He raised his eyebrows. "Could have been nothing,

though."

"Follow me." Ted led us to the stairwell. "I found this tacked on the wall." He handed me a sheet of paper.

On it was written: "Payment is coming due."

I shoved it at Heath. "So collect already. I'm getting tired of dancing." I stomped down the stairs leaving the men to follow. "He's playing games. Taunting me. Trying to catch me off guard. Then, he'll pounce like a lion on a gazelle." My stomach rolled. I had no way of knowing when and where the killer would strike. What I did know was that I wasn't going to sit back and wait helplessly.

To an onlooker, I might have appeared mad and brave, but inside, I quivered like the last leaf on a tree, caught by winter's frigid blast. I wanted to run and hide. Instead, I'd soldier through, try to stay alive, and hopefully catch my father's killer.

I wasn't a crime solver, I was a gardener, but no matter how hard I tried to convince myself, life had something else in mind. One murder after another set me off on a dangerous path at regular intervals. How lucky could a girl get?

"Shelby, stop." Heath swung me around and into his arms. "I won't let anything happen to you."

"Then you'll fall with me."

"Then I will." He peered intently into my face. "What affects you, affects me. We're in this together."

"I hope the two of you like company," Ted said, his face grim. "Because I've just become your new bodyguard."

"I guess I'd rather have a retired cop than an old lady," I said into Heath's chest. My cottage was going to be rather crowded.

"What did I miss?" Grandma hurried toward us as we emerged from the building. "My instincts are humming."

"We were trapped in the elevator and Ted is our new bodyguard," I said.

"Oh, goody. It'll be like a twenty-four hour party." She glanced at our faces. "Should we be worried about Sue Ellen?"

"We shouldn't take any chances," Ted said. "Shelby, looks like you'll have someone besides you in your bed. Ida and I will take the guest room, Heath the sofa. It'll be tight, but this is the way it should be until this person is caught."

"He only wants me." I squared my shoulders. "He'll never get close if I'm constantly surrounded, nor will I be able to find out who he is. Besides, Cheryl is coming tomorrow night. Where is she going to sleep?"

"Let me think for a moment." Ted stared over my shoulder. "You made some good points, but leaving you unprotected is like using you as bait."

"No way." Heath shook his head. "At least let me stay, Shelby. With Cheryl there, it won't seem out of the ordinary to anyone watching. We can reinstate the security system you shut off after Christmas."

"I hate that thing. I never remember to set it." So, rather than have to remember, I'd canceled the service.

"It's either that or you have a cottage full of people." He raised his eyebrows.

"Fine. Call the security company." It looked like, if I wanted to catch this killer, I'd have to break a promise to Heath and sneak away at some point. I wouldn't risk his life for my own vengeance.

I'd have to pray he'd have the chance to forgive me.

9

*C*heryl woke me the next morning by jumping on my bed. "Hey, since when does Heath sleep on the sofa?"

"Shouldn't you be at work?" I pulled the blankets up.

"I called in sick. Get up and tell me everything." She yanked the covers off me.

I groaned and sat up. When I finished telling her about everything that had happened, including yesterday, her eyes were wide and her mouth open. "So, Heath is staying here. If you don't have a problem sleeping in here with me, I can give him the guestroom."

"Not a chance." Heath stood in the doorway, a coffee mug in each hand, and a smile on his face. "Staying in the living room puts me first in the line of sight to anyone breaking in."

"Thanks." I took the coffee and patted the mattress

beside me. "There's always the back door."

"You don't have a habit of leaving that one unlocked." He grinned. "I'm here to lock doors and windows, stay between you and the bad guy, kiss you goodnight, and bring you coffee in the morning."

Cheryl sighed. "I think I want Seth living with me if he'll bring me coffee in bed."

I laughed and leaned against Heath. "Sorry, but God broke the mold with my man."

"Maybe." She gave a little bounce, almost spilling my coffee. "So, what are we doing today to catch this person who is out to get you?"

I glanced at Heath, who watched me. "Uh, well, I think I need to talk to Mom first thing. We were thinking about speaking with some of the officers Dad used to work with."

"Sounds like a plan." She blew into her mug. "I took a discretionary day on Monday, so I'm all yours for four days."

"Give me an hour or two to get some things done on my to-do list." Heath stood. "The two of you stay together and don't leave the premises. I'll find you when I'm finished and we'll get started."

The moment he left, Cheryl grabbed my hand. "Are you really going to sit back and wait?"

"For now." I swung my legs over the side of the bed and padded on barefeet for the bathroom. "But, we will go talk to Mom, at least."

"Ugh."

I laughed and closed the bathroom door. I'd play it safe as long as Cheryl was with me. We'd been in dangerous situations together too many times. This time, I couldn't endanger my loved ones. I *had* to do this on my own.

~

"I want to be involved with this one," Mom said the moment we stepped up to her desk.

"With what?" I asked.

"Seth told me that the person after you may have something to do with your father's death. I've wanted vengeance for five years." She cast a steely look on me. A look more scary than the "Mom" look she used to give me on a regular basis.

"I don't want you in danger."

"That's my decision. Either we work together or I work on my own. I know you think I'm soft, but underneath this lady-like exterior, beats the heart of an Amazon." She lifted her chin. "So, partners?"

"Don't forget me." Grandma jumped from around the corner. "I knew something was up the moment Sue Ellen left her cottage. She doesn't usually walk with such a determined stride."

Cheryl glanced from one to the other of us and grinned. "I love this family." She held out her hand. "All for one and one for all?"

We piled our hands on top of hers. Tears stung my eyes. Come hell or high water as they say, we were in this together.

"Room for a man in that women's club?" Heath's gaze locked on mine.

I let the tears fall and nodded. "Just don't get killed."

"I'll do my best. Here's to the Shady Acres crime solvers."

"I like the sound of that," Grandma said. "Maybe we should start our own detective business. I wouldn't mind taking pictures of cheating scoundrels and charging them instead of their grieving wife."

We laughed and gathered around a round table in the foyer.

"We need the names of the men Dad worked with." I handed her a sheet of paper I'd pulled from the printer.

"I'm not sure I can remember them all, dear, but if not, the ones I can will fill in the blanks." Mom started writing. When she finished, she slid the paper back to me. "I'm going with you."

"I know. You've made that very clear."

"I don't think they'll talk with all five us."

"The rest of us will wait in the car," Heath said. "We're only there for backup. I'm finished for the day, if you're ready to go."

Mom nodded. "I already told Alice I needed the afternoon off. She wasn't happy, but I threatened to quit, so she caved."

"Smart woman." I folded the paper and slid it into the pocket of my jeans, then followed Heath to the only vehicle big enough to carry us all. Grandma's van.

I ran to ride shotgun, and chuckled as she complained that she had the right to sit up front in her own vehicle. Still grumbling, she climbed in back and scooted to the middle.

"There's no room back here with Cheryl. She's too big."

"Are you saying I'm fat?" Cheryl screeched.

"No, I said you were big. Which you are." Grandma glared.

"Let's go," I told Heath. "Before World War III starts in the backseat."

He drove us to a small bungalow on the outskirts of town. "First house." He cut me a glance. "I'm here if you need me."

"Thanks, but I'm not afraid of a retired officer." I shoved open the door. "Mom?"

"Coming." She joined me. "I remember Larry Johnson. A gentle giant. Him and his wife joined us for dinner a lot when you were small."

"The African American couple?"

"That's them. I heard she died last year of cancer. Very sad."

"You should have told me."

"I sent flowers." She pressed the doorbell.

The door opened. The largest man I've ever seen stood there, a stern look on his round face. He stood well over six feet and had to weigh three hundred pounds. When his gaze landed on Mom, he smiled. "Sue Ellen. It's been a long time."

"Yes, Larry, it has. May we come in?"

"Why sure." He stepped back and ushered us into a meticulous room with dark leather furniture. "Have a seat and tell me what brings you and little Shelby to my home." He lowered his bulk into a chair.

Mom bit her lower lip. "This is difficult, but Shelby has found herself the target of an unscrupulous someone who we believe may have been involved in James's death. I'd like you to tell me everything you can about my husband and what he was involved in."

"I'm not opening that door and neither should you." He rested his elbows on his knees and leaned forward. "I'm serious, Sue Ellen. James wouldn't want you to put your life at risk."

"Shelby's life is already at risk. Either you help us

or we find someone who can." Mom leaned against the back of the sofa. "You were his best friend. His partner at one time. I can't believe you're turning your back on me."

I never realized how thick Mom could lay on the guilt. I settled back and prepared myself to watch the show. Poor Mr. Johnson didn't stand a chance.

"I'm doing the exact opposite. I am helping you by not giving you the information you want. You have no idea who you're dealing with."

She tilted her head as if he were a child having a hard time understanding a lesson in manners. "The Yellow Jackets?"

"Where did you hear that name?" His eyes turned to slits.

"I found it in some files my father left behind," I said. "That's when we first realized his death was not a random accident. Someone is trying to kill me, Mr. Johnson. I'd like to find them before that happens."

"Please don't be the cause of me losing another family member, Larry." Mom's voice trembled.

Boy, she was good.

"What other files did you see?" Larry shook his head, his large hands now dangling between his knees.

"No, sir." Mom gave a sly smile. "You only want to find out what we know so you can give us very little else." She shook her index finger at him.

Who was this woman? She could have been a spy she was so cool. I'd never been more impressed with her in my life.

"When did you become such a hard woman, Sue Ellen?"

"When my husband was shot dead in the street

because of expired tags."

He sighed. "In the middle years of James's career, he worked undercover, infiltrating a gang run by Carmen Sanchez's father. When Carmen grew up, he left and formed his own chapter, calling it Yellow Jackets. They're cold and ruthless. Young men who think nothing of killing in cold blood. Right before his death, James found out the location of Carmen Senior and alerted the FBI."

"He was still working on the gangs?" Mom's face paled. "He never said anything to me."

"He was detecting on his own, Sue Ellen. Something he should never have done. He didn't tell me until two days before his death. I urged him to take you and Shelby and get out of town. That's how dangerous these people are."

"He did ask me to take a vacation. He suggested I take Shelby to Disneyland. I refused, saying we couldn't afford to." She swiped the back of her hand across her eyes. "Thank you for telling me this. Now, where can I find this Carmen Sanchez?"

"I won't tell you that." He crossed his massive arms and sat back in his chair.

"Do you know the name Harvey Weston?" I asked.

"He was an accountant for Sanchez. Went into Witness Protection."

"That we know." I leaned forward. "Who is his son?"

"How are you finding out this information?"

"That's our business, Mr. Johnson. Do you know his son?"

"Not personally. The boy's name was Sean. He'd be about twenty-five now, I think. Dark hair, blue eyes.

Why?"

"Harvey was killed in prison last week. I'm the reason he was sentenced. Whoever is after me keeps saying I owe a debt. My guess…Harvey's son is the one after me."

"Then he isn't a Yellow Jacket. They don't allow whites into their ranks."

I twisted my mouth and thought for a moment. Could it be possible I was looking for two people? The one after me, and the one who killed my father? If so, which did I concentrate my efforts on?

If I looked for my father's killer, I could die. If I searched for the person who wants me dead, Dad's killer goes free another day. I rubbed between my eyes where a headache was starting.

I decided I was going after Dad's killer. If I died, I died knowing I had done what I could to bring him justice. "Tell me where the Yellow Jackets hang out."

"Nope." He shook his head. "I will not be a part of it."

"Larry." Mom did her head thing again. "Would you rather we wandered the streets at will, having no clue where we're going? What if we happen into enemy territory?"

"That's what I'm afraid of!"

Mom stood. "Then I guess we'll start asking on the street corners of the inner city. It was nice seeing you again." She headed for the door.

Mr. Johnson groaned. "They hang out in Harrisburg on York Street. God help us all."

10

*O*nce we headed for the van, I turned to Mom. "When did you become such a manipulative interrogator?"

"Since my two sisters were born after me." She grinned. "As the oldest, I learned a lot of tricks on how to get the information I needed in order to blackmail them."

"You're pure evil." I laughed. "Are we headed for the next guy on the list or straight over to Harrisburg?" Before she could answer, my cell phone rang.

"It's me, Alice. Get back here at once. Someone broke into your cottage." Click.

"We gotta run." I sprinted for the van. "Someone broke into my cottage," I told the others as soon as I leaped into the front passenger seat.

Heath didn't hesitate. The moment Mom's door was closed, he roared toward Shady Acres as if more than my privacy had been violated.

Forty-five minutes later, we raced toward my humble abode where Seth and Ted stood. Seth glanced at the four of us, narrowed his eyes, then waved a hand toward the front door. "Let's see what's missing."

Thank goodness Seth had taken Dad's box to the station already. I stepped into chaos. Furniture ripped and overturned, cabinets opened, pictures askew. I trudged to the bedroom where I found my mattress slashed and shoved off the bed. Strewn around the room was clothing from the dresser and closet. Yep, someone was looking for Dad's box.

"Tell me it's safe." I cut Seth a sharp look.

"Locked in the evidence room. Anything missing?"

"I don't think so, but clearly it wasn't for lack of trying." I shoved against my ruined mattress. While tears clogged my throat, all I could think of was it could have been worse. None of the furniture was actually mine. The cottage had come furnished.

Heath wrapped his arms around me from behind and rested his chin on top of my head. "I'll get this cleared out and bring you replacements from storage."

"Thank you." I turned to face a rapidly approaching Alice.

She shooed the others from the room and slammed the door. "When corporate hears about this, they're going to want to fire me. Again!"

"I didn't ask for this." I started picking up my clothes.

"You never do, but my job is at stake, Shelby." She clutched her ever-present clipboard to her chest.

I straightened and stared. "Are you going to fire me?"

"Just asking you to take a leave of absence while things die down. Like maybe…six months?"

"Are you crazy!? I can't afford that. This is my home."

Cheryl burst into the room. "You can't fire Shelby because your boss blames what's happening around here on you. That's ludicrous."

"The residents signed a petition, Alice." Something didn't add up. A visit to the corporate office in Little Rock was in order.

"They didn't care about the petition." She refused to meet my gaze.

"What's really going on?" I tossed a shirt toward the closet.

"Nothing."

"Alice." I practically growled her name.

"Oh, very well." She righted the chair in my room and sat down. "I want a raise and they won't give me one because of the expensive repairs that result every time you have a murder to solve. Painting, cleaning up blood," she waved her arm, "new furniture. The only good thing about it all is that we stay fully booked."

"So, this is all your idea? The bottom dollar?" I'd heard it all. "You want me gone until you get a raise?"

"Yes, yes, and yes. I'm sorry. I'm shallow, I know that."

"I'm not leaving, Alice." I leaned until my face was inches from hers. "Listen up, girlfriend, and I really did think we were becoming friends, you stop harassing me over things I have no control over, or I'll sic my mother on you. She just made a giant of a man give us information he wanted to keep hidden."

Ooops. Seth glanced at Mom.

"I'm not afraid of Sue Ellen," Alice said.

"You should be." Mom stepped forward. "Lay off Shelby or I walk, my mother walks, Heath walks, Ted walks, and Shelby walks. Then what are you going to do? You've lost tenants and workers."

"Fine!" She lunged to her feet. "Just...clean this place up."

She clomped away in her usual ungraceful in heels way of walking.

"Wow." I sat in the chair she'd vacated. "I didn't expect that."

"Don't worry about her," Mom said, patting my shoulder. "She'll realize someday that money isn't everything."

"She's just jealous." Grandma studied her manicure. "I heard her talking to someone on the phone the other day about how we have our little click that solves mysteries together and we never invite her to join. She thinks she should be invited because she's the manager."

"I've let her come along before." Once, Alice had almost become a victim. Would I have let her help if she hadn't? Probably not. I could only take her in small doses.

"True, but I might have let slip that we actually have our own little club." She had the courtesy to look ashamed. "And that the name was the Shady Acres Gumshoes."

"We never said that was the name." Mom shook her head.

"We have to have a name, Sue Ellen. We tossed around ideas, but someone had to make a decision."

"I cannot believe I'm wasting time listening to

this." Seth pulled a notepad from his pocket. "Tell me what this giant of a man told you. What's his name?"

"Shelby has a big mouth." Cheryl stepped closer to him. "It was nothing."

He stared into her eyes. "You stayed in the van, didn't you?"

She sighed and stepped back. "Yes."

"Sue Ellen?" Seth tapped his pencil on the paper.

"I'd rather not. It's just speculation, Seth. I don't want to spread rumors."

"Either you tell me or I arrest you for impeding an investigation."

She spilled her guts. "We thought Harvey's son might have a connection with the Yellow Jackets. He doesn't because they don't let in white people. We know they're in Harrisburg, and we know that Harvey was an accountant for someone named Sanchez. There. See? It isn't that much."

"I thought you had more sense than your daughter." Seth paled. "You want to talk to Sanchez, don't you?"

"If we can find him."

"No one knows what he looks like. He sends out his orders via text on a burner phone." He snapped the notepad closed. "This is over y'all's head. Heath, keep them out of this." He stormed away.

Heath's gaze focused on me. "We're dealing with gangs?"

My shoulders slumped. There was no way he'd let me continue.

"Speaking with the officers my father worked with was your idea."

"Yes, but questioning a violent gang boss is not."

A muscle ticked in his jaw.

"Heath." Alice yelled down the hall. "Our new resident needs help moving into number thirty-one."

"This isn't over, Shelby." He turned and left.

I glanced at Ted. "What now?"

"I'm not letting Ida get mixed up in this."

"You aren't letting me?" Grandma's brows lowered. "Are you my boss now?"

"Don't take that in a way it wasn't intended." His face darkened.

"Then how was it intended? We are out to find justice for my son-in-law. If we have to snoop in dangerous territory, then so be it. Besides, who is going to harm three women? Sure, they might give us a warning or two, but I seriously doubt anyone is going to kill us."

"Then you're a fool." He stomped away.

"Well," Cheryl said. "You ladies managed to alienate your men. What do we do now?"

"Order a pizza," I said. "This is going to take a while to clean up. I don't think it's on Heath's priority list anymore. Maybe when we've finished, we'll have a plan."

I flipped the mattress over to the undamaged side and slid it on the boxed springs. "Before we head into Yellow Jacket territory, I want to speak with the other officers on that list."

"Hello?" Scott's voice rang down the hall. "Sue Ellen? I have a package for you. Alice said you were here."

"Down here, Scott."

"Whoa." He froze in the doorway.

"Just a little mishap." Mom smiled and took the

box from his hands. "I'll see you later, all right?"

He nodded, glanced at each of us, and started to say something. Then, apparently thinking better of it, he went in the same direction as the other men.

"I ordered tracking devices." Mom placed the box on the bed and opened it with a key from her pocket. "They look like diamond earrings. I want us all to wear them at all times."

"What a great idea!" Grandma grabbed a pair. "Sue Ellen, you do surprise me sometimes."

"She's been surprising me quite a lot recently." I took my pair and slid them into my ears.

"All we have to do is link them to an app on our phone and we can keep track of each other 24/7. You can find all kinds of things on the internet." Mom's eyes sparkled as bright as the fake diamonds she was putting in her ears. "They had a very high rating. Just make sure your phone is charged and turned on."

Oops. I was lucky if I remembered to take my phone if I was sprinting out the door. "You want to do this despite Heath and Ted saying no?"

"Yes, Shelby, I do. I really want to close the case on your father so I can move ahead with my life." Her eyes shimmered. "I really like Bob, but I can't envision a future with him until this is settled."

"What if we fail?"

She lifted her chin. "We won't. But, if we do, we can proudly say we did our best and didn't quit. After this, I plan on never investigating anything again. It's too stressful."

I was more worried about losing Heath. He'd made it quite clear about me going into danger against his will. Still, I understood what my mother was saying.

Dad's death haunted me, too. It was time to put an end to the questions.

11

*W*hen I hadn't heard from Heath by the next morning, I went looking for him. I found him rolling a dolly loaded with boxes into cottage number thirty-one. A handsome Hispanic man stood with arms crossed and watched. I never would understand why some people thought working men were their slaves.

As I approached, Heath spotted me and stopped pushing the dolly. "Good morning, Shelby." He gave me the warm smile that melted my heart. Missing was the usual twinkle in his hazel eyes. Instead, a flicker of sorrow shined.

"Do you have a minute?"

"Excuse me, Mr. Perez." Heath took a step toward me.

The man glanced at his watch. "Make it quick. I've business to attend to."

Heath sighed and led me to a clump of bushes.

I glanced back to see Mr. Perez's dark gaze fixed on us. "He doesn't seem very nice."

"He's rude. What do you need, Shelby?"

"Are we okay?" I searched his face for anything to still my troubled heart. Heath had to be out of sorts if he had an unkind word to say about a man he'd just met.

"We have to be, don't we? I want you in my life, craziness and all." He ran his hands through his hair. "I just need a little time to process the fact you're going to face a gang leader."

I wanted to say he didn't have any time, that I needed him to do this with me, even if only by giving his support. Then, I caught a vision of him slain by a gang member's bullet. I needed to make sure that didn't happen. Foolish on my part or not, I felt a woman might be a little safer in this instant. "I'll give you the space you need." I turned to go.

"Wait." He turned me to face him. "I'm not asking for a separation, or space, or a temporary reprieve. I'm just asking for the time to process this. Give me a day or two. I don't want you solving this without me."

Tears stung my eyes. "You aren't break—"

"Hey." Mr. Perez yelled from in front of his cottage. "Time's up."

Heath rolled his eyes. "I'll see you at lunch. I doubt I make it to breakfast." He gave me a soft kiss on the lips and rejoined the new tenant.

I headed for breakfast determined to solve this case before Heath had a chance to join me in the investigating. It was bad enough I had Mom and Grandma. Then Cheryl. I could lose any of them and life would never be the same.

"Why the long face?" Cheryl jogged to my side.

"I don't want anyone else involved in bringing down Dad's killer." I swiped my hand across my eyes. "It's too risky for them."

"Too late." She linked her arm with mine, not an easy task because of her height. It caused her to walk bent over and lean heavily on me. "We love you, so we help you. You're the bravest person I know, but you also spend the most time worrying about the what ifs."

"If not for me, no one would be involved with danger. We'd each rattle along, happy in our blissful ignorance."

"Really?" Her eyes widened. "You planned on finding that dead woman your first day on the job? What about the following cases? You plan those, too? Or," she held up a finger, "what about your father? Did you plan for him to be shot during that traffic stop?"

"Of course not." I pulled away from her, my blood boiling. "What's your point?"

"My point, little girl, is that you didn't ask for any of this. We volunteered to help you as these things, these deaths, this danger, came up and affected all of us in one way or another. So, like it or not, we're all in this together." Cheryl tossed her mane of blond hair over her shoulder and marched to the diningroom.

I stared after her. Was she right? Was I trying to keep them back when they wanted to help me as much as I wanted to keep them safe? Head hanging, I trudged after her. If my loved ones insisted on entering the lion's den with me, I'd have to be more careful about making foolish choices. Which could slow things down.

Glancing to my right, I spotted Scott and Mr. Perez in a heated discussion. Then, they both looked my way and headed around the corner of the building. I shook my head, not wanting to get involved in their drama and opened the diningroom door.

Cheryl must have told Mom and Grandma about our conversation outside, because all three heads swiveled when I approached the table. "Fine. Come with me or not. It's your skin on the line."

"Finally, she's gotten wise." Grandma toasted me with her mimosa.

I rolled my eyes and headed for the buffet. Mr. Perez entered and got in line behind me. "Good morning," I said. "Welcome to Shady Acres."

He flashed a dentist-whitened smile. "Thank you. It seems to be a fine place," he answered in a thick accent. "I look forward to many years here."

I asked Joyce for a ham and cheese omelet. "I love when you do made-to-order omelets."

"You like all of my cooking." The chef grinned.

Steve Olsen, the newest addition to the kitchen staff, stepped from the kitchen. His eyes widened when he spotted Mr. Perez, then he ducked back out of sight. Curious. The normally shy man wasn't usually that degree of shyness. I glanced over my shoulder. Mr. Perez seemed not to have noticed as he pointed out the items he wanted in his omelet.

Again, I chose not to invest in someone else's drama. I had plenty of my own. Instead, I gratefully joined my family at our usual table.

"Now that we've got the foolishness of Shelby thinking she's responsible for our welfare out of the way, we have plans to make." Grandma rubbed her hands together. "Where do we start?"

"We finish talking to Dad's old friends. Someone, somewhere, has to know something about Carmen

Sanchez." I cut a bite of my omelet, pleased at the string of cheese stretching from the fork to my plate.

"So, that means we all stay in the van while you and Sue Ellen question people." Grandma pouted.

"Pretty much." I winked at Cheryl.

She frowned. "I agree with Ida this time. I didn't take off work to sit in a van that smells like…the kind of powder old people wear."

"I don't wear powder!" Grandma clunked her fluted glass on the table. "That's a delicate French perfume. I paid thirty dollars for the bottle."

"Thirty dollars too much." Cheryl popped a mushroom into her mouth.

"Stop fighting." I straightened in my chair. "You act like children. We can't all converge on these retired officers. They'll feel ganged up on and won't talk. They'll talk to Mom because of Dad. I'm the one someone tried to kill. The two of us do the questioning. End of subject."

Grandma sniffed. "You sure grew up bossy."

After breakfast, the four of us climbed into the van. I texted Heath that we were leaving, but he said Alice had him doing an emergency repair on her toilet. I then texted him the link to the app to put on his phone so he would have our tracker information.

I drove, making Grandma happy by letting her ride in the front seat. We pulled into a neighborhood that had seen better days. The small bungalow type homes were in need of painting and updating. Some of the yards were so overgrown, the driveways were hidden under years of dirt and weeds.

"Charles must have hit on some bad luck," Mom said, opening her door. "He always said he was going to inherit some money and spend his retirement years well off. I wonder what happened."

"Let's find out." I led the way up the cracked and buckled sidewalk and knocked.

After a few minutes, a heavy-set man with red eyes and whiskey-ladened breath opened the door. I took a step back and breathed slowly. I didn't think he'd bathed in a month.

"Charles Baker?" Mom held out her hand. "I'm James Hart's widow."

"Who?" He frowned and blinked.

"Officer James Hart. May we ask you a few questions?"

"About what?"

"The day he was killed."

He slammed the door in our faces.

I glanced at Mom, brows raised, and knocked again. A bullet blasted a hole in the door, missing me by inches. I dove into the bushes on one side, Mom the other.

"I think he knows something," I yelled to her.

"I agree." Mom reached over and knocked again. "Stop that, Charles. This is important. Shake off the drunken stupor and talk to us."

"Go away before I do more than a warning shot."

"I'm trying to find out the truth about my husband's death. Please talk to us."

The door opened. "Hurry up before someone sees you."

Seriously? He didn't think the gunshot caught anyone's attention?

"Do you want me to call the police?" Grandma shouted out the van window.

"No!" Mom called back, stepping into Baker's house.

If I thought the man smelled bad, the house was like the inside of a garbage can that had sat closed up with fish and chicken inside. I gagged and did my best to compose myself. I couldn't. "Can we please talk outside?"

"No." He shook his head. "I've managed to stay alive and hidden for years. Now you two show up and put me at risk."

"From whom?"

"Yellow Jackets." He grinned. "Now, unless you have some bug spray, I got nothing to tell you."

Mom scratched her eyebrow, a sure sign she was thinking. "If you help us pin James's murder on them, then you'll have all the bug spray you need."

"I can't do that."

"Why not?" I crossed my arms. "What aren't you telling us?"

"Look, girl. Your daddy died doing something he believed in. I let him go alone that day. No, I didn't know he'd be killed, but if I hadn't had too much to drink the night before, he wouldn't have been alone. Instead, I showed up at the station, two sheets to the wind, and they sent me home on suspension. I've blamed myself every day since for his death."

"You knew he was in trouble?"

He nodded. "We were getting close. Real close. So close we could almost see Sanchez's face."

"That doesn't explain why you feel as if you need to hide," I said. "You aren't telling us everything."

"Fine. I took some money from Sanchez to turn the other cheek during a drug deal. Then, I felt guilty and squealed. To your father."

"Then you owe it to us to help." I crossed my arms. This man was indirectly responsible for my father's murder. If he wasn't so openly suffering, I'd shoot him.

"Hold on. I've got some photos here somewhere." He bent over a stack of papers on the coffee table.

The van horn honked long and loud outside. Instead of the front, the sound came from the back of the house.

The front window of the house shattered.

I grabbed Mom and threw myself on top of her.

I glanced over to see Baker on the floor with a bullet hole between his eyes.

"Find the photos!" Mom texted something into her phone.

I dug through the scattered papers, finally giving up when another bullet came through the wall. Instead, I grabbed them all, then took hold of Mom's hand, and raced through the kitchen and out a back door.

Grandma had the van waiting in the alley.

We piled in and raced away.

My hands shook. Nausea roiled in my stomach.

"Keep an eye out for a golden Impala," Grandma said. "I got suspicious when it drove up and down the block a couple of times. Cheryl and I stayed ducked down in our seats, but when it drove by real slow, we took the first opportunity to leave the street and warned you."

"I'm very much obliged. This is why we need someone waiting outside." I leaned against the seat back and fought to steady my breathing. "Take me to the nearest copy store, then the police station." I'd behave responsibly and turn the photos over to Seth, but I'd make copies first.

I shuffled through the papers in my hands, locating several grainy, black and white photos. It would be hard to ID anyone from the poor quality shots, but maybe once we had time to study them a bit something would jump out at us.

"He had to have been looking at these when we showed up," Mom said, glancing over. "But why? Why would a man so eaten up with guilt keep feeding the flame?"

I shrugged. "My guess is that Larryy warned him. Which means the others will be expecting us too."

"Seth wants us to come straight to the station," Mom said.

"You texted him?"

"Yes, as soon as bullets starting flying, so drive fast so we can make those copies. He said if we weren't there in thirty minutes, he was putting an APB out on us."

Grandma stepped on the gas, rocketing us down the freeway.

12

*W*ith copies of the photos safe in Grandma's big bag, I carried the others inside the police station. The receptionist took one look at me and sent me down the hall.

Hmm. She was usually friendlier. She wasn't the only one to give us strange looks.

One officer stopped us. "Do you need help?"

"No thanks." I stepped into Seth's office.

"For crying out loud!" Seth stood and slammed the door to his office. "Have you looked in the mirror, Shelby? No wonder the photoshop guy called the station about a couple of strange women. Hand over the copies and the originals."

I frowned. "What's wrong with me?"

"You're covered in blood and…flecks."

"Oh, my gosh! Oh, my gosh!" I started jumping up and down and flapping my arms. "Get it off!"

"You need a shower, dear." Mom grabbed a tissue from a box on Seth's desk, licked it, and attempted to clean my face.

I grabbed Seth's trashcan and threw up. Now, blood didn't usually cause this reaction in me, but I'd never been covered in someone else's before either. "I need a therapist. I'm traumatized."

"We have a shower, that's the best I can do for you," Seth said, the corner of his mouth twitching, "but you'll have to wear orange. We don't have extra street clothes lying around."

"I don't care. Where is it?"

"All the way to the end of the hall. Turn left, last door on the right. Ignore any ribald calls coming from the holding cells. Then, come straight back here to give me a report."

"I had no idea this station was that big."

"We used to be a smaller version of our prison, until other cities outgrew us. We still have some of the amenities." He waved a hand as if to usher us away faster.

As Mom and I left the room, I heard Grandma telling him she had no idea where I put the copies. Seth would find them for sure once he demanded to look in her bag.

"You made two copies, right?" Mom giggled.

"Yep. The other set is stashed under the driver's seat in the van." I turned the corner at the end of the hall.

Immediately four men from a cell started whistling and make suggestive comments.

"Look straight ahead," Mom said. "Don't acknowledge them. That encourages their behavior."

Some of the things they said left me feeling like I needed two showers and to soak in a tub of bleach. How did Seth work with these types of people day in and day out? It would sour me on humanity.

We stepped into the shower room. My heart plummeted to my feet. Five shower heads in one large open stall lined a tiled wall. It was the nightmare of high school gym class all over again.

"I'll turn my back while you shower, then you can do the same for me," Mom offered, handing me a large towel. "While I've seen all you've got, it's changed a bit since you were a baby."

"Thanks. You're the best."

I stripped, rolling the soiled clothes into a ball and shoving them in a nearby trashcan. I couldn't wear those sweats again. Not ever. I turned on the shower, stood back while the water got hot, then stepped under the spray, loading my hands with soap/shampoo from a dispenser on the wall.

I closed my eyes at the sight of red-tinged water swirling around the drain at my feet. When I was certain I'd washed every trace of Charles Baker from my body, I wrapped the thin towel around me. "Your turn." I snatched an orange shirt and pants from a shelf on the wall and got dressed while Mom showered.

The clothes hung on me. Even with the drawstring pulled as tight as possible around my waist, the pants almost fell off.

Mom showered and dressed and stared at me with her lips pursed. "Not exactly a fashion statement."

"Better than what we were wearing. Let's go give Seth that report." I linked arms with her and ignored the laughter from the inmates on our return trip past their cell.

Seth's eyes widened when we entered his office, but he wisely kept his mouth shut. Not so with Grandma.

"You two look ridiculous. Orange is not your color." She pointed at Seth. "He took the copies from me."

I shrugged. "Let's do this. We have more people to interview."

"Dressed as an inmate?" Seth laughed and sat in the chair behind his desk.

"Of course we'll change first." I glanced around the room. "Where's Cheryl?"

"Went to get coffee. She said you always drink it when you're stressed."

I love that gal.

Mom started talking, giving Seth information from the moment I knocked on Baker's door to when we dashed out the back. "That's it."

He folded his hands on the desktop. "Charles Baker didn't quit the force, he was fired for taking money. He was a dirty cop." He shook his head. "I hope he's telling the truth about wanting to come clean. I hate when a cop dies dirty." He spread out the photos on his desk. "Do you recognize anyone in these photos?"

"No," I said. "The quality is too bad. Can you get them enhanced?"

"Maybe." He pierced me with a sharp glance. "You know I won't be able to share any information with you."

"A girl can always hope." I looked up and grinned as Cheryl entered with a tray of coffee mugs.

"What did I miss?" She sat on the corner of Seth's desk.

"Just your boyfriend being obstinate." I sipped my brew. Just the way I liked it. Full of creamer. "We told him everything. He told us nothing."

"I sent a unit to Baker's house. There's really nothing to tell you that you don't already know. You were there." He exhaled sharply. "Again, I'm not crazy about how close you women came to getting killed. But, I give up."

"Don't worry." Grandma patted his cheek. "We won't ask you to cry at our funeral or give the eulogy. Let's go home and get you two out of those uniforms. It's almost lunchtime."

"Please don't let me catch you out and about without Ted again. I assigned him as your bodyguard for a reason." Seth wrote something on a piece of paper in front of him.

Cheryl sighed when we left his office. "Silly man refuses to kiss me at work."

"It isn't professional." Mom hitched up her pants and grinned at the stunned receptionist as we strolled out the front door.

The van exploded.

The concussion sent us flying backward. I slammed into the red brick of the building.

~

I opened my eyes to the sight of a strange man wearing a white coat shining a light in my eyes. Had someone finally had me committed?

"Miss Hart? I'm Doctor Sheldon. You took quite a knock to the head and broke a couple of ribs. You'll feel every bruise by morning. How are you feeling right now?"

"Relieved."

"Excuse me?"

"I thought I was in the psyche ward." I scooted to a sitting position.

"Do you need to be?" His brows disappeared into his hairline.

"Definitely." Heath stood from the chair he'd been sitting in and moved to the bedside.

"You're here." I took his hand.

"I wouldn't be anywhere else." He brought my hand to his lips.

"How's Mom? Grandma? Cheryl?"

"They're fine. Your mother landed in some bushes, so her landing was a bit softer than yours. Ida ended up in the fountain, and Cheryl on top of her. Your grandmother is sputtering about Cheryl almost drowning her, then crying the next minute because the van is gone."

So were the extra copies of the photographs. But, the main thing was that we were all alive.

"I'll leave you alone," Doctor Sheldon said. "Press the button on your handset if you need the nurse. I'll be back in a couple of hours to check on you."

"I want to go home."

"In the morning." He gave a patronizing smile. "We'd like to keep you overnight for observation."

I pulled my hand free from Heath and slapped the mattress after he left. "I hate hospitals."

"You flew a few feet into a building, Shelby. Spend the night." Heath pulled the chair closer to the bed and sat down. "Are you thirsty?"

I nodded and he lifted a plastic cup with a bendable

straw to my mouth. Once I'd wet my throat, I asked, "Where's Seth?"

"Going from room-to-room like a worried mother hen. He feels responsible since it happened at the station."

"That's silly. They shouldn't have to check every vehicle parked in the lot for bombs." But it would have been nice since the police knew someone was out to get me. "What set it off?"

"They don't know yet." He took my hand again and rubbed his thumb over the back. "But they suspect the bomb was under the hood."

"The trigger?"

"No idea. The engine was cool by the time you came out, according to Seth. He said you were there at least an hour."

I closed my eyes. What I had feared might happened, almost did. I could have lost my family right along with myself. Still, I wouldn't have known that if I were dead. I wouldn't have had to live with the fact they were gone. Maybe it was better, thought my selfish mind, to keep them close.

"You're awake." Seth rushed into the room. "Are you okay? I just came from Sue Ellen's room. She's sharing with Ida. Neither one of them are happy. Cheryl got lucky enough to have her own room also."

"I'm fine. Any clues?"

"Not a one, but it's the Yellow Jackets's style. With further investigation we believe they detonated from an outside location."

"You mean they were watching us." My blood ran cold.

"Yes."

"They're still playing games." What's their purpose? Why not kill me and get it over with? Oh. "They're looking for something." I focused on Seth. "What did you find in Dad's papers that I missed?"

"There's a list of undercover cops working within the ranks of the Yellow Jackets. The list wasn't in the file. Which means…"

"They think I have it." But where? What would the list be on? A jump drive or a disc? Written down? I was pretty sure it wasn't in my cottage, which meant…I needed to search Mom's house. The one I grew up in and Cheryl now rented.

"Tell Cheryl not to go home. She has to stay at Shady Acres. Tell her to take a leave of absence from work. The gang has to know about my mother's house. Cheryl isn't safe there."

He nodded. "I'll tell her. I'll have the doctor write up something saying she needs medical leave." Worry shadowed his eyes. "I'm doing my best to keep y'all safe, but you sure make it hard." He placed a hand tenderly on my shoulder. "See you in the morning. Earlier if I find out anything. We'll have an armed officer at your door and your family's."

"Thank you. I'm heading to Mom's house the minute I'm released from here."

"Text me. I'll meet you there."

I watched him leave, then turned to Heath. "Find someone that knows bombs who is willing to scope out my mother's house once we're released from here. I've some searching to do and don't want police interference."

"Are you sure?" He cleared his throat. "Let Seth find the list. He's better equipped to know what to do once he finds it."

"Heath, no. I don't want anyone but Seth involved. When Sanchez does come for me, I'd better have something to trade for my life and the life of my loved ones. If I can't promise him the list, use it to stall him, I'm already dead."

13

*D*octor Sheldon was right. I hurt everywhere the next morning. If not for Heath's strong arms I wouldn't have been able to get out of bed. Searching Mom's house would have to wait until I could move more than two feet without leaning heavily on Heath's arm.

Outside the hospital Ted waited with a shiny new Dodge Caravan and a big grin on his face. "Will this do, Ida dear?"

Grandma clapped her hands. "Oh, yes! It's perfect."

The new van was a definite improvement on the one that got blown to pieces. Rather than ride back in the van with the others, Heath helped me into his truck and buckled my seatbelt. "Are you all right? Do you need anything?"

I cupped his cheek in my hand. "I'm fine. Thank you." I felt gratitude for much more than I could put into words and tried to convey all that I was feeling with my eyes. It worked in the movies after all. Characters read words of love from a simple heavy-eyed stare.

"You have two black eyes," Heath said, a dimple winking in his cheek. "My little raccoon."

So much for romantic eye gestures. "I'm sure I have more than my eyes that are black and blue."

He gave me a quick kiss and jogged around to the driver's side. After sliding into his seat, we followed the van back to Shady Acres. Once there, we made our way, three of us limping, toward my cottage.

Seth waited out front. "Sue Ellen, your house has been broken into. Cheryl, thank God you weren't there. The place is trashed." He gave her a quick hug, then jumped back as if one of the other officers might be around.

I glanced at Mom and smiled. I knew why the place had been trashed and other than worry over what might be broken, didn't despair too much. "No worries, Seth." I patted his shoulder on the way inside.

"Explain." He followed us inside and crossed his arms. "Who isn't worried about their home being ransacked?"

"Settle down." Mom sat on the sofa next to me. "That house was built during the Prohibition. There are so many hiding cubbies that no one can find anything unless they know where to look. If James hid that list in my house, no vandals, gangs, or transients will find it. Shelby probably knows that house better than anyone other than her father."

"If it's there, I'll find it." I high-fived Mom.

"This is the weirdest family I've ever worked

with." Seth kissed Cheryl then stormed out the door.

"Wow, my man is so romantic." Cheryl plopped down next to Mom, leaving Grandma one of the easy chairs. Ted took the other and Heath straddled a kitchen chair.

We sat around and stared at each other for several minutes until I started to grow uncomfortable. "What is no one saying?"

"We're just itching to go search, but I for one can't move without my muscles protesting," Grandma said. "Teddy, I need some wine."

"It's ten a.m."

"I know what time it is, sweetie, but it's a most effective pain killer."

He closed his eyes for a second, then stared at her. "I will not get you tipsy so you can disobey doctor's orders and not take it easy."

"You sure know how to ruin a girl's fun." She pouted. "What are we supposed to do all day?"

"We could spend time coming up with a game plan rather than go forward like headless chickens."

"That sounds like a great idea," I said before the two of them got into a full-fledged argument. "Heath, there's a clipboard and paper in the drawer next to the fridge."

He jumped up to get it. "I'll also start coffee before you ladies fall asleep."

Sleep actually sounded more wonderful than coming up with a plan. While maybe not the most responsible thing, heading off on spur of the moment searches made life more exciting. I closed my eyes.

When I woke, dusk was falling and someone had covered me with a blanket. Heath snored from a nearby chair.

"Where is everyone?" I sat up.

"You four ladies fell asleep, so Ted went home. He'll be back with supper. Did you get a nice rest?" He ran his fingers through his hair, then over his face.

"Yes, it appears you did, too." I grinned. "Sorry about that. I know we were going to jot down notes."

"We can do that this evening just as easily. I think everyone was more tired than they wanted to admit."

A knock sounded at the door.

Heath pushed to his feet and peeked through a slit in the curtains. "Supper time." He opened the door.

Ted entered with plastic bags of Chinese takeout. "Food's here."

As if he'd rang a bell, Mom, Grandma, and Cheryl shuffled from the bedrooms.

"You read my mind." Cheryl took one of the bags and pulled out cardboard boxes, setting them on the coffee table.

Mom headed for the kitchen returning with plates and utensils. "I never could master chopsticks."

After a few minutes of nothing but eating, I spoke, "Does Seth know we're going ahead with trying to solve this?"

Ted nodded, using chopsticks to drop a noodle in his mouth. "Yep. He's not happy about it, but short of arresting all of us, he doesn't have a choice. And, since I'm your bodyguard, I can't very well not tag along, now can I? Ida named me an honorary member of this so-called Shady Acres Gumshoes."

"Welcome aboard. You'll be a valuable member." I set my plate on the coffeetable. "Answering from a law enforcement officer's viewpoint, what's the next thing you would do?"

"Find that list." He speared me with his gaze. "Then, I'd finish interviewing your father's contacts. Don't face the gang unless you have to. If you find irrefutable proof of what happened without heading into hell, then you can hand it over to Seth and be done."

I liked that plan. While I was determined to bring Dad's killer to justice, not facing a gang leader sounded good. I glanced at Mom to gauge her reaction.

She stared at Ted for a moment, then nodded. "I agree. I suggest we visit Larry Johnson again regarding Baker, then move onto the next. After we search the house."

"Of course." Ted turned to Heath. "Do you agree?"

I loved how the older man often deferred to my man. Heath might be a handyman, but he had a good head on his shoulders and more empathy than anyone in the room. If there was a kinder way of doing something, he would find it. If there wasn't, then he would do what was necessary. "I think you should accompany Sue Ellen to speak to Johnson this time. Maybe he'll tell another retired officer what he wouldn't say to her alone."

"So, you think he knows more than he told us?" I asked.

"Possibly. They were all part of the division assigned to bringing down the gangs. Which means, they had to have at least suspected, if not known about, Baker's deception." Ted sat back in his chair. "Cops know more about each other than they let on. If these men were close, they may have tried to bring Baker around without turning him in."

"Except they were too late." My throat clogged.

"Yes, if my speculations are correct, and that's what they are, Shelby…speculations."

"Let's carry this conversation to the hot tub," Grandma said. "My muscles could use a soak."

That actually sounded like a good idea. "Meet back here in fifteen minutes."

"Remember," Ted said. "No one goes anywhere alone. Heath, come with us. We'll stop by your place on the way."

It wasn't until Ted stood up that I noticed the gun on his hip. When he'd arrived, the bags of food had caught my attention. I was relieved to know Ted was watching out for Heath as well as the rest of us.

Once they left, and I'd locked the door behind them, I headed for my room and my swimsuit and robe. The hot tub might feel nice, but the air would be freezing. I wasn't a huge fan of hot tubs, the temperature gave me a headache, but I knew they wouldn't leave me behind, which meant if I didn't go, no one would go.

I got into my modest one piece royal blue bathing suit and covered it with a fluffy terry robe. Feet slipped into thick slippers, I grabbed a bunch of towels from the linen closet and met the other women in the living room. It took closer to thirty minutes before the others returned.

"Sorry," Ted said. "Your grandmother couldn't decide which bathing suit fit the situation. She has way too many."

"We're involved in a mystery, Teddy. So, I needed a mysterious suit. I chose black with scarlet red lipstick. Very avant garde." She grinned, waving a glass of wine.

I figured that was the real reason for their tardiness. I seriously doubted it was her first glass. I wasn't a prude or a tee-totaller, per se, but sometimes Grandma worried me. "No glass allowed in the pool area."

She scowled at me and grabbed a plastic cup from my cupboard. "Happy?"

"Just following the rules."

"Since when?"

I shrugged, smiled, and headed for the front door.

Ted stopped me with an outstretched arm. "I go first. Always."

"I'm second." Grandma sailed out of the cottage, the rest of us following.

"She gives me gray hair," Mom said. "I often wonder who's the parent. Her or me."

"Me, too," I laughed as Grandma opened the gate to the pool area.

She strolled inside the gate and almost immediately dashed back out and into Ted's arms. "In the pool." She pointed.

Mom and I glanced at each other and rushed through the open gate.

Floating face down in the pool was Alice, her blond hair spread around her like a halo highlight blue from the pool light. "Oh, no. Heath." I held out my hand for him to grasp.

He bypassed my hand and pulled me into his arms. "Why her?"

"I don't know. Maybe it's not related to whoever is trying to kill you."

"It is." I knew it in my gut. I pulled back and peered into his eyes. "Whoever this is, has been playing a game, but I could have been killed in the greenhouse that day. What changed? Was the greenhouse not meant to kill me? What possible connection could Alice have?

"I've called Seth," Ted said, his arm around Grandma. "There's a whiskey bottle next to the pool. Maybe she had too much to drink and fell in."

I jerked. "She didn't drink. Anyone who knows her, knows that. She followed the rules exactly and never did anything she thought might jeopardize her job. Whoever killed her didn't know her very well."

"Come sit over here." He tried leading me to a table.

I pulled free. "No. I need to get into her office. She made notes of everything." And I did mean everything.

He pushed me into a chair. "Not now. You aren't going anywhere until Seth and the police arrive. I won't have you in the pool next to Alice."

"She's really dead." I covered my eyes with my hands and cried.

14

"*I*t's a mannequin," Seth said, pulling the body from the pool by its hair.

"What?" I took my hands from my eyes. Looking closer, I couldn't believe I'd thought it was Alice. Still, the blue light of the pool and the gentle ripple of the water had helped deceive us. That and the fact I expected a dead body around every corner. "Then, where's Alice?"

Seth waved a hand to Officer Wayman to check her office and her apartment. "What made you think it was Alice?" He asked, turning to me.

"That's her black pencil skirt and she's worn that yellow blouse plenty of times." Not to mention the blond hair that had floated around her. "I knew you wouldn't want us to touch the body, so…"

"Right." He didn't look as if he believed me about the not touching part. For good reason, I supposed. I'd probably contaminated a crime scene more times than I could count. "Somebody wanted you to believe it was Alice."

A text came through on my cell, alerting me with a ding. I pulled it from where I'd stashed it in the pocket of my robe. "Message left in my office. I know you can find it. Figure it out. Throw this phone in the pool immediately."

So I did. It fell with a plop next to Seth.

"What the heck?" Seth jumped back as if bitten. "What are you doing?"

I shrugged and raised my eyebrows. Obviously Alice needed me to find something and didn't want Seth to know. I wasn't about to betray that trust. At least not until I had a chance to see what the message might be. But then again, I doubted I'd be able to go to her office without him.

"Shelby, come with me." Seth motioned toward the gate.

I cast a look for help at Heath, who nodded and followed. Once outside the gate, I spoke softly, "I cannot explain here. The phone slipped. That's all you need to know right now." Especially since I still thought it was someone common to Shady Acres behind all this. Someone who might be listening at that very moment.

Seth's eye glittered in the light of a nearby lamp. "Got it. Stay close."

Those of us who had wanted to soak in the hot tub, sat on the patio furniture until Seth and his team had cleared the area for us to leave. By then, I yawned more than not and leaned my head on Heath's shoulder while staring at my phone in the bottom of the pool. I loved that phone.

Officer Wayman used the long-handled pool scooper net thingie to fish out my phone. He shook the water from it and handed it to me. "I seriously doubt it will work."

"I think you're right." Alice had better have a darn good reason for the order. Funny how I went from despair to annoyance in regards to her. I'd bought a new phone a few weeks ago, sparing no expense on the bright pink case.

When the authorities had finished with the area, Seth told me to come with him. I was starting to get tired of being ordered around. He put his foot down when the entire family wanted to come, even telling Ted to stay back with Mom, Grandma, and Cheryl. Only Heath was allowed to tag along.

He led us to his squad car and told us to get in. Once in, he turned to me, "Alright. I figured out you were afraid of someone overhearing us. No one can hear you in here. Why did you throw your phone in the pool?"

"I got a message from Alice, I think, saying she left me a message in her office and to throw the phone in the pool. I'm assuming it's because the phone would be ruined and no one could retrieve the message."

Seth blinked a few times. "Any clue where she's hiding?"

"No, and I have no idea how she'll contact me in the future. Can the phone be fixed?"

"Maybe." He held out his hand. "I'll take it in and see what we can get from it." He studied the phone, then laughed. "You have it in a protective case, Shelby. It's fine."

"I don't remember buying that…oh. I wondered why the case was so expensive. The guy at the phone store said it was the best case. Alice didn't expect that, I guess."

Seth shook his head. "And you let her have a gun, Heath?"

"She forgets it most of the time, much like her phone."

"Let's get over to Alice's office and let Shelby do her snooping." He pushed open the door. "Something she's quite good at, I have to admit."

"My phone?" I held out my hand.

"Nope. Not until we see if we can find out where Alice is hiding."

I growled deep in my throat and waited for him to open the door to the backseat. After sliding out, the three of us trooped to Alice's office.

I stood in the doorway and surveyed something similar to the aftermath of a tornado. Someone had been there before us. Still, she wouldn't have sent me the message if she believed someone had taken what she wanted me to find. I moved to the desk and stared down at her blotter. She'd jotted down a to-do list and several phone numbers. I ripped off the top sheet, folded it, and slid it in the pocket of my robe.

"Don't touch anything else." Seth handed me a pair of latex gloves. "I got these from the kitchen. Now, you may proceed."

"Thanks, boss." I pulled on the gloves and dug through the garbage can, pulling out anything with names, numbers, or a note that didn't make sense.

"Can we help you look?' Heath asked.

"No, I won't know what I'm looking for until I

find it. Thanks, anyway." I moved to the filing cabinet.

"Sometimes, I think you'd make a good police officer," Seth said, "then at others, I'm glad you aren't. I don't think society could handle Shelby with authority."

I rolled my eyes and kept looking. Ah ha! Tucked under the files was a little black book. Kind of obvious, but it too went into my pocket. An hour later, I thought I had everything that might be a message.

Then, I stared straight into Seth's eyes. "For whatever reason, Alice entrusted this task to me. Short of hauling me to jail, I will not turn over what's in my pocket until I find the message she left."

He stared back, no expression on his face, and gave a small nod. "My condolences, Heath." Then, he led us back to my cottage where the others waited.

"Spill your guts," Grandma said. "No secrets here."

"There should be," Seth said. He perched on the arm of the sofa next to Cheryl. "I need a date with you."

"I'm in agreement. Tomorrow night? That Italian food place?"

He nodded.

"Are y'all going to make personal plans or help me find out what Alice wanted me to find?" I grinned, then glanced at Heath who winked.

I spread everything I'd found over the coffee table and stared at a whole lot of nothing that made any sense. "I guess we could call the phone numbers and see whether they're legit."

"Maybe the notes are in code," Grandma suggested." 1 for A, 2 for B, etc." She grabbed a slip of paper with a phone number and deciphered gibberish.

"That isn't it."

"Let me compare the numbers to residents at Shady Acres," Mom said. "We might be able to discount some of them and make cold-calling easier."

"Great idea." I grinned and handed her everything with anything resembling a phone number. As for the black book, it contained nothing more than birthdays.

"Hmmph. I would have thought of that eventually," Grandma said, scowling.

"It isn't a competition, Grandma." I glanced at the clock on the wall. "I suggest we get some sleep. My body is hating me right now. Let's meet here at eight to head over to the house."

I fell asleep praying for Alice's message and Dad's hiding place to jump out at me.

~

By nine o'clock, we all stood in front of my childhood home and waited while Mom stepped first through the open front door. She clapped a hand over her mouth and staggered back.

Seth and Heath stepped in front of her and entered, me right on their heels. I pushed between them.

Trashed was an understatement. The house was vandalized. Furniture stuffing ripped, books off the shelves, dishes shattered, even the ashes from the fireplace were not where they belonged.

Tears sprang to my eyes. Sure, these things could be repaired, they were material after all and the house itself was fine. I took a deep breath and moved inside.

"I'm sorry, sweetheart." Heath put his arm around my waist. "What can we do?"

"Guard the doors. We can't have anyone watching." I marched to the fireplace and ran my hands down the right side of the rock. When my finger slid into a crack in the plaster, I wiggled it, then stepped back while the wall slid out enough for me to squeeze through and head down a set of steep wooden steps.

"Shelby?" Heath's voice followed me.

"I'm fine." I lit a lantern on the dirt wall of the cellar with a match from a nearby jar and carried it deeper into the room.

During Prohibition, the shelves on the walls had held moonshine and homemade wine. In later years, Dad had stored important papers there. For something of the magnitude of a list of undercover cops, no shelf would work. I needed a more secret place.

I skirted around a few toys and faded blankets from when I was a child and the dark room was the Beast's lair and I was Belle. When I reached the end of the ten-by-twelve-foot cellar, I turned. Where could someone hide something small?

"Shelby?"

"Still okay, Heath."

"We have company."

"Everyone down here. Quickly." My heart sat in my throat as they all squeezed into the small room.

Grandma looked around. "Huh. Never would have guessed this was here. I hope they don't set the house on fire."

"Hush, Mother." Mom glared at her.

I rushed up the stairs and pulled the lever that slid the wall back into place. "If we're quiet, they'll never find us."

"I lived here for years and didn't know about this room," Mom said. "I guess my husband had some secrets."

"I caught him going in here once, when I was little and couldn't sleep. I often roamed the halls at night. I never told him, but I'm sure he figured it out when he saw my toys."

Footsteps and raised voices overhead quieted us as efficiently as a hand over our mouth. I agreed with Grandma. I prayed they wouldn't burn the house down.

Cheryl's eyes widened as the footsteps headed for the bedroom. "My school records. They contain the names and addresses of my students."

Seth made a chopping motion with one hand. In the other, he clutched his Glock. "Shh. They aren't after your students."

I couldn't make out what our visitors were saying, but they didn't sound happy. After all, Seth's patrol car and Grandma's van were parked in front of the house. A clear sign that someone was here. People didn't vanish into thin air.

Dust rained on my head. Not only were they in the house, but someone patrolled the outside. The cellar didn't reach under the house.

I glanced to the overhead light...and smiled. Dad had installed a dome where once there had been only a bare bulb. I tapped Heath on the shoulder and signed for him to give me a boost. Once I sat on his shoulders, I removed the screws holding the dome in place and handed them down.

Then, I peered into the dome. Nestled inside, wrapped in dingy white fabric was a small rectangular object. I dug it out and unwrapped a jump drive. "Got it," I whispered.

Heath patted my leg. "Good job." He lowered me to the ground.

Now, if only I could figure out Alice's message as easily.

The voices grew louder again as the footsteps moved closer, stopping at the fireplace. Eyes glued to the rock wall above us, I prayed. We stood shoulder-to-shoulder in that cellar. If they set the house on fire, we'd be trapped down there with a room quickly filling with smoke.

Without making a sound, we watched as the first tendrils of grey smoke wafted between the rocks of the fireplace and footsteps pounded away. The worst thing that could have happened...did.

"I hate when I'm right," Grandma said, leaning into Ted.

I pulled my tee shirt over my nose, slid to the floor, tugging Heath with me, and started praying.

15

"*I*t can't be very bad yet. The fire just started." Seth bounded up the stairs.

"It could be a trap." Cheryl reached for him, just missing the hem of his shirt.

He glanced back at us. "That's a chance I have to take. Ted, shoot anyone that enters except me."

"I've got my gun, too." Grandma dug it from her bag. "I'm ready."

God help us all. "Please don't shoot the wrong person, Grandma." I coughed and pulled my shirt tighter over the bottom part of my face. "I'm sorry about the house, Mom." Tears streamed down my face, whether from the smoke or sadness, I wasn't sure, but I suspected a bit of both.

Seth squared his shoulders and pulled the lever. The door opened and he stepped out, gun drawn.

Someone yelled.

A gunshot rang out.

A cry.

Seconds later, Seth reappeared. "Coast is clear. They left one guard, a stupid kid, who built a fire in the fireplace. I took him out of commission when he pulled a gun on me."

Eyes streaming, I followed him out, the others right behind me. I mentally added fixing the chinking in the fireplace to my to-do list. The room had never filled with smoke before, and I'd spent a lot of chilly winter mornings curled up with a book in the cellar.

Sitting on the floor against the wall, a rag tied around the bullet hole in his leg, was a young Hispanic man wearing a yellow Tee-shirt. He couldn't be more than seventeen.

Coughing and hacking, we all sat on whatever flat surface we could and stared at the young man who glared back.

"Did you get any information from him?" I asked.

"No." Seth squatted in front of the him. "Ready to talk?"

The young man spit, hitting Seth in the chest.

"That is about the rudest thing I've seen in a long time, and believe me, in my years as a teacher I've seen some things." Cheryl marched to him and towered all five-feet-eleven-inches of her over the now wide-eyed gang member. "You change your attitude right this instant or I'll drag you to the station by your ear. Got it? How cool do you think you'll be then?"

Go, Miss Leroix. I bet her students didn't act up too much when she brought the hammer down.

"Now, get up and march to the squad car before I drag you." She pointed outside.

"I'm shot in the leg."

"And whose fault is that? Get. While you're in jail, I expect you to think about the path you've chosen for your life."

"Yes, ma'am." He struggled to his feet and, with sweat pouring down his face, limped to the squad car.

Looking very satisfied with herself, Cheryl wiped her hands on her pants. "Would you like me to interrogate him, Seth?"

Stunned, he shook his head. "No, we don't want him getting off because of brutality. I'll meet y'all back at Shady Acres when I'm finished. Shelby, the jump drive."

I handed it over. "I'll get a blank one from the store and make up names to go on it. I need something to turn over if I'm taken."

"Don't get taken." He turned to Cheryl. "You truly are an Amazon. My Amazon." He pulled her close for a kiss, then caught up with our young gang member who had stopped to rest next to a porch post.

"Well, that's that." Mom glanced around the room. "It'll take a month of Sundays to set this place to rights again."

"Not if we all pitch in." I righted a chair.

Soon, the rest of us put things back where they belonged, tossed what was broken, and had the house liveable again. Cheryl headed upstairs to get her files.

"I may not have reason to stay on medical leave," she said, "but I do think I should sleep at Shady Acres until this case is put to rest."

I agreed. Now, to focus on figuring out Alice's message.

~

With promises to bring back lunch for me, everyone but Heath headed to the diningroom, leaving the two of us to stare at the papers strewn across my coffeetable. "I don't see anything resembling a secret message."

"If you did, it wouldn't be secret." Heath bumped me with his shoulder. "Let me see the black book."

I handed it over. "Mostly odd numbers."

"This one looks like an address." He opened my laptop and started typing. "It's the address to a motel off Interstate 40."

"Do you think Alice is hiding there?"

"It's possible." He scribbled a note telling the others where we'd gone. Taking my hand, he led me to his truck. "This might be a dead end, but we have to start somewhere."

Twenty minutes later, he pulled in front of a white clapboard motel, single story, in the shape of an L. We headed to the manager's office.

"Have you seen this woman?" Heath showed a picture from his phone.

I frowned. "You have a picture of Alice on your phone?"

"I have a picture of every person I have a phone number of." He looked at me as if to say, *doesn't everyone?*

The clerk studied the picture. "Yeah. But she's gone now. Left this morning."

"Did she say where?" Heath asked.

"Nah, and we don't ask. As long as they pay their bill, we don't care."

"Has her room been cleaned?" I leaned on the counter. "We're helping the police with an investigation."

"Like private eyes?"

"Exactly." I grinned.

"No, the room hasn't been cleaned. Come on." He snagged a key from a pegboard behind the desk.

We followed him to room 31. "She requested this room. Said it might be important to someone."

I glanced at Heath. "She knew we'd come looking for her."

"Tony Perez lives in cottage 31."

"Coincidence?"

He shrugged. "I doubt it. He must be linked to this somehow."

The manager unlocked the door and stepped aside. "Just pull the door closed behind you when you're done."

Heath closed and locked the door. "I'll take the bathroom."

I nodded and glanced around the room. Newly renovated, but still not above a 3-star hotel in my estimation. A generic white blanket lay folded at the end of a bed covered with white sheets. A rust-colored chair sat next to a round table. Tan curtains covered the window.

I knelt beside the bed and glanced under. Not even a speck. I moved to the nightstand…nothing, then the dresser and checked all the drawers inside and along the edges. Still nothing. There had to be something. Alice wouldn't have us follow her here to leave nothing. I pulled the dresser away from the wall.

Bingo. Taped to the back was a pink post-it note. On it was written "Lincoln Foster."

"Heath, I need your cell phone."

He handed me his phone and I typed the name in his search engine. "Lincoln Foster was the town's recluse in the early 1900s. He lived on Cooper Mountain." I glanced up at Heath. "Why would Alice give us his name?"

"I guess we're headed up the mountain to find out. Let me alert Seth to Perez and number 31."

After Heath made the call, nodding and saying "uh huh" several times, he hung up. "Seth says to definitely not go snooping around on the mountain without him. There are still people up there who think they're living in the nineteenth century and don't like trespassers."

"Then what do we do?"

"Head back to Shady Acres, I guess. Someone has to run the place in Alice's absence."

"Mom can. She knows where everything is anyway."

We did a quick check to make sure we didn't miss anything and left.

"That's Scott."

He wheeled a dolly full of boxes into the manager's office. When he came back out, his steps faltered at the sight of us standing there. "Hey, Shelby…Heath." His gaze flickered to the door behind us.

"Oh." My face heated. "It isn't what it looks like. We're just following a lead." Gracious. I hoped the man wasn't a gossip. I'd never live down the humiliation. Mom would disown me.

"What kind of lead?" He kept looking around us.

"Well, Alice has disappeared. She didn't say anything to you, did she?"

Heath stepped on my toe.

"Ow." I tossed him a dirty look.

"No, I rarely spoke to Alice. Most of the time I only see Sue Ellen." He turned an unsmiling gaze on me. "You did ask her not to snoop, right? It seems like she's snooping."

"I told her." Why was it so important to him? Sure, he liked my mother, but he almost acted as if it were his duty to warn her away. I tilted my head. "What do you know, Scott?"

"About what?"

"Someone trying to kill me."

He sighed. "Absolutely nothing." He rolled the dolly past us and to his truck.

I wasn't sure I believed him. "Thank you for your concern, but I can take care of my mother."

I could have sworn he muttered, "I doubt it." He turned and smiled. "See you back at the nuthouse." He climbed into his truck and rumbled away.

"Why did you stomp on my foot?" I turned on Heath.

"I didn't stomp, and you were talking too much." He took my arm and led me to his truck. "What do you really know about Scott? I worked with him for a few weeks, remember? I don't know much about him despite that. You said it had to be someone close that hooked that generator up to the greenhouse. I agree."

"Scott isn't close. He's there once a day on the days we have a delivery. Someone would have noticed him"

"Not necessarily." Heath waited until we were both in our seat before continuing. "Shady Acres is surrounded by forest. All it takes is someone who knows their way around. A person could easily come up to the greenhouse from the woods and not be seen unless someone was close by. No one ever goes there but you."

True. I wrapped my arms around me for warmth, suddenly cold. "What would he have against me?"

"What would anyone at Shady Acres have against you?" He turned onto the Interstate. "I'm not saying it's Scott. I'm saying for you to be careful with what information you share. I agree with you that if we find out who Harvey's son is, we'll find out the person who tried to kill you."

Not easily done with all the other things that pull us away from finding out that one important fact.

Heath's cell phone rang, connecting to the Bluetooth in his truck. Very cool.

"This is Heath McLeroy."

"It's Seth. I thought you guys might want to know that no one has seen Tony Perez in two days. And…no one had seen Alice at all yesterday, except for Birdie. She said she saw her heading toward the tunnels. Meet me at Shady Acres. I need into the tunnels." Click.

Heath glanced at me. "Could she be hiding in there?"

"Maybe at first, but I doubt she's there now. If Perez knew about them, he could have used them to get away without anyone seeing him, I guess." Chances were slim on that account.

The tunnels weren't used for anything other than a storm shelter anymore. After a killer had chased me through there, we kept it locked. Perez would not have had a key. "If Alice did go to the tunnels, I'm thinking she may have left us another clue."

"The question is…why is she investigating alone?"

I knew the answer to that one. She wanted so desperately into our club that she'd solve this mystery to prove her worth.

I prayed her desire wouldn't get her killed.

16

*H*eath unlocked the heavy door leading to the tunnels. "You first, Seth. You're the law, after all."

"Here." Seth handed me my phone. "Alice used a burner phone to text you."

Figured. I hung back. I'd had enough of that dark, dank place to last me a lifetime. To try and stay out of sight, I stood in the shade of a giant magnolia tree while the men searched. As I did, I studied the treeline behind the greenhouse. It would be very easy for someone to come that way and not be seen.

"Heath, I'm checking out something. Hello?" When he didn't respond, I knew he was out of hearing range. My resolve wavered. Should I check things out on my own or wait? Standing around accomplished nothing. I had my Tazor in my purse, I'd be fine. I hoped. It would be great to find signs but not the actual person who left the signs.

With the occasional glance over my shoulder in case Heath emerged, I set off for the trees. A few yards in I found two sets of footprints. Both size eleven with different treads. Were their more than one crazy person after me? One sole sported a popular zig zag pattern, the other squares. I squatted next to them and snapped a picture with my cellphone. I was starting to feel like a bonafide private eye.

Until a stick snapped somewhere behind me. Then, I was nothing more than a chicken. I bolted to my feet and spun around in time to see a squirrel scamper across my path.

I chuckled and glanced back the way I'd come, making sure the greenhouse was in sight. I couldn't see the entrance to the tunnels, but knowing Heath and Seth weren't that far away spurred me on. If I needed to scream, they'd hear me, hopefully.

I didn't expect to find anything else, not really. The gas and garden hose used to try and kill me were the same type as the ones used at Shady Acres. Same with the generator. But, I felt positive the killer sneaked on the grounds by this path. I needed to see where it led.

I sent Heath a text telling him where I'd gone and continued walking at a leisurely pace in case the men wanted to catch up. Which they would. Most likely the second Heath received this text. I smiled at the thought of my gallant knight rushing to my side.

The path curved, taking me out of sight of Shady Acres. I squared my shoulders and kept going. No point in stopping now. What if the path led me to the person responsible for my problems?

Oh! What if the path led me to the person

responsible for my problems? A good or bad point, depending on how you looked at it. My legs threatened to buckle. *You can do this, Shelby.* Why was I so brave surrounded by others, wanting to save everyone, then when I managed to get off on my own I turned into a helpless ninny?

I wasn't helpless. I was working hard to stay alive and find justice for my father. Yes, that sometimes caused me to step into unsafe situations, but the reward would be wonderful once I reached my goal.

I was so deep in thought, I found myself on the side of the road leading to Shady Acres before I realized I'd stepped from the trees. It didn't tell me who was after me, but it did let me know how they had gotten to me. Anyone could have parked there and gone for a murderous jog.

Scott's delivery van pulled to a stop a few feet from me. He stared at me through the front window for a few seconds, then rolled down his window. "Need a ride?"

"How far is it from here?"

"About a mile."

I took my bottom lip between my teeth, tempted by the ache in my feet. "No, I shouldn't. Heath is right behind me. If I'm not here, he'll be worried."

"Suit yourself." He rolled up his window and headed down the road.

I found a relatively smooth rock the size of a camping stool and sat down to wait. There sure weren't many cars that went down this road. I guess other than the occasional delivery from Scott and whoever brought the groceries, the residents would be the only ones with business down here. Which—in my mind—confirmed the wanna-be-killer was someone I knew.

Still, there was also the question of where Tony Perez had gone to. Was his disappearance connected to Alice's? What if Tony had become a victim? This case was suspiciously absent of dead bodies. In the past, I'd already stumbled over one or two by now. Not that I was complaining. Not at all. I was actually glad. Still…

"There you are." Heath burst from the trees. "You gave me a scare, Shelby. I've asked you not to go anywhere alone."

"I had to know where this path led." I held up my hand for him to help me to my feet. "Where's Seth?"

"Examining the items we found in the tunnels."

"Like what?"

"Bottled water, dried food, that type of stuff. It's almost as if someone thought they might be camping out in there." He grinned. "What makes us think it was a probable place for Alice was the makeup."

"A place for her to hide if she ran out of others. No clues?"

"No. I don't think she's been there other than to stash food and water."

"She's running scared, Heath. She had to have found out something that put her life in danger. I need to go through the things I took from her office again."

"That will have to wait. Seth is ready to head up the mountain. He's asked your mom to have Joyce fix us a lunch."

I grinned and grabbed his hand. "Well, what are we waiting for?"

~

In order to attract less attention by the locals, we took Seth's civilian Ford Taurus rather than the squad car. Grandma and the others were not happy about being left behind and let us know it by threatening to tie themselves to the car's bumper. Well, only Grandma threatened that action, but the others' scowls said plenty.

I gave a jaunty wave as we drove from the parking lot. Grandma's wave wasn't as nice. I turned back to the front seat. "Not to be a pain, but I'm pretty sure Lincoln Foster is dead by now."

"I agree." Seth looked at me through the rearview mirror. "But, if we find the cabin, we most likely find Alice. I doubt the person after you two would know who Lincoln Foster is."

"Unless they found the name, left it behind the dresser to lure me to them, googled it, and are waiting to ambush us."

He shook his head. "Possible, but not plausible. Halt the imagination, please."

"My imagination is what helps solve these cases."

"She has you there," Heath said, laughing. "Shelby thinks outside the box."

"Do you know where we're going?" I leaned over the seat. "If Lincoln didn't want his cabin found, we won't find it."

"I found the old deed. I know exactly where it is."

Half an hour later, Seth drove down a rutted road. Weeds scratched the bottom of his car. Tree branches reached out like witches trying to snatch a child in some macabre fairy tale.

I shuddered at the thought. "How much further?"

"We get out and walk from here." Seth stopped the car and shoved open his door. "There doesn't seem to have been any recent travel on this road. That's a good sign that no one is waiting for us."

It could also mean Alice wasn't there and we'd wasted our time, but I wisely kept my mouth shut. Instead, I grabbed the backpack with the food and water, which Heath immediately snatched from me, and slid from the car.

"How far?" I eyed the flat soled tennis shoes on my feet. Not exactly hiking wear, and I already had the beginnings of a blister from my previous jaunt through the woods.

"Want a piggyback ride?" Heath asked, smiling.

"Yes. No." I sighed. I refused to be the baby of the group. What I really needed was a crime solving bag. In it would be my gun, poor thing that was always forgotten on the top shelf of my closet, my Tazor, water, socks, a couple of granola bars, and a sturdy pair of comfortable hiking boots.

After what seemed like an eternity, and after the forming blister on my foot decided to start screaming, we stepped into an overgrown clearing. In front of us was a ramshackle log cabin. You could see through holes in the walls where the chinking had fallen out. The porch steps sagged, and the fireplace looked ready to fall down. It definitely looked uninhabited.

"Stay behind me," Seth said, drawing his pistol. "We're going inside."

My steps faltered. I clutched my Tazor. That was the type of house spiders liked. I hated spiders.

"I'll protect you," Heath whispered in my hair. The man knew me so well.

"Good." I shuddered, and stepped into the cabin behind Seth.

Someone was living there. A propane campstove

rested on the table, a sleeping bag and pillow lay on the floor, and a propane heater sat a few feet away. But the clue that told us for sure Alice was the camper was the pair of turquoise blue stiletto heels poking out from under the sleeping bag. She'd wised up in regards to footwear it seemed, having left her heels behind. Surely she wasn't walking barefoot. At least in the woods, she might have chosen something more sensible to wear.

"Where do you think she is?" I peered through a hole in the back window shutter.

Leaves crunched outside.

Heath pulled me behind him.

Seth held his gun at the ready.

The door opened.

"For crying out loud, Seth, put that away." Alice glared. "It's about time you found me." She set a bucket of water on the floor next to the table. "I left enough clues."

"In scattered, far off places," I said, crossing my arms. My gaze dropped to the running shoes on her feet. "Now, explain yourself."

"Didn't you figure out the number 31?" She waved to a couple of three-legged stools.

"Yes. It has something to do with Tony Perez," Seth said. "Why don't you tell us what you know and how you know it without us dragging it from you syllable by syllable?"

"Fine." She rolled her eyes. "I was doing a bit of…research on the newer residents of Shady Acres. You know, after Shelby said she thought it was someone close to her that hooked up that hose. Anyway, I happened across Tony Perez. Now, his driver's license checked out and a preliminary credit report, we have to do those to lease, but if you dug a little further into his background…there wasn't anything. It's as if the man didn't exist. Now, I've watched plenty of crime shows on television. I know what that means." She wiggled her eyebrows. "Tony Perez isn't his real name."

"Go on." Seth narrowed his eyes.

"So, I have a friend who is a crime scene technician in St. Louis and I sent him a picture of Perez's driver's license. Now, it's not a confirmed match, only a suspected match, but we believe Perez is actually Carmen Sanchez." She smirked. "Can I join your club now?"

"Definitely." I was impressed.

"So, we now know what the gang boss looks like, and what they're after, but why would he want to kill me? That carbon monoxide would have done the trick and the gang wouldn't have any chance of procuring the jump drive. What's the debt I have to pay?" I glanced from face-to-face. "I still think it's the son of Harvey. How do we find out who he is before he gets to me?"

17

Seth tucked his tongue into his cheek, then nodded. "I have an idea. If Perez really is Sanchez, then this could be correct. Harvey and his son went into Witness Protection because of the gang. Your father was killed by the gang." He paced the small living room. "So, if I can get someone from the FBI to dig up the son's identity based on what we know…"

"Then we'll know who he is." Hope sprang in me. This case could be coming to a close.

"We need to put Alice into protective custody," Seth said. "With Perez in hiding, she is definitely in danger."

"I'll stay here." She glanced at each of us.

"No, we need you under guard. Take what you need. We'll find a safe house."

I couldn't help but wonder if she was still excited about being a part of the Shady Acres Gumshoes. I almost asked why I wasn't in protective custody, then remembered I was, sort of. At least as much as I would allow. Everywhere I went either Seth or Ted were there. "It isn't so bad, Alice. Maybe they'll have a handsome officer watch over you."

She rolled her eyes and grabbed a backpack from next to the front door. After shoving the stilettos inside, she said, "Let's go then. You can watch over me at work."

"I think it wiser to put you somewhere else." Seth gave her a stony look. "Sue Ellen is handling things at home."

Alice narrowed her eyes. "I insist."

"I'm the authority here, not you."

I smiled. Alice finally found someone she couldn't bully into submission.

Alice stomped her way to the Taurus. Seth still didn't waver in his decision.

I couldn't remember the last time I'd been so entertained. Grinning like a loon, I climbed into the middle of the backseat so Alice couldn't sit next to Heath.

Seth dropped us off at home, before leaving to take Alice to wherever it was he thought she'd be safe. "I'll call you tonight," he told Cheryl before turning his car toward the road.

"Sometimes I don't know why I fell in love with a cop." She watched the Taurus leave the parking lot. "I worry every time he drives away."

"You should do what I did," Grandma said, linking her arm with Ted's. "Grab them after they retire."

I laughed. "I don't think Cheryl wants to wait that long."

"Definitely not." Cheryl smiled. "I'm nearing thirty and really want a couple of kids of my own."

We turned to head for the dining room.

An engine revved behind us.

We turned.

A black Suburban cut off the Taurus. The window rolled down, a semi-automatic weapon sprayed the Taurus with bullets.

My eyes widened as I watched the horror play out in front of us. The others seemed as stunned as I was. It wasn't until Ted pulled Grandma to the ground that the rest of us thought to do the same. Except for Cheryl.

Cheryl screamed and grabbed Grandma's purse. As she raced toward the shooters, she pulled Grandma's gun from the purse and fired a shot of her own.

The Suburban peeled away.

I got to my feet and chased after Cheryl, Heath and the others right behind me.

"Call an ambulance!" Ted shouted, reaching for the driver's side door of the Taurus.

Cheryl put a hand over mouth, dropping the gun at the sight of Seth covered in blood.

Mom pulled out her phone.

Heath yanked open the passenger side door and felt for a pulse in Alice's neck. "Weak, She's been shot a few times."

"So has Seth," Ted said. "Do what you can to stop the bleeding."

I shrugged out of my hoodie and handed it to Heath. *Please, God, spare them.*

While the men worked to save the lives of our friends, I moved to the edge of the parking lot to watch for the ambulance. I wanted to do more, but knew I'd only be in the way. How foolish of us to think we could escape the gang that controlled the next town. The gang that had killed my father and now wanted what I had. That thought had me stepping back a few feet. But, if the gang wanted me dead, I'd have been killed long before now.

I spotted the ambulance approaching and waved my arms.

They roared into the parking lot. No sooner had they stopped, then the back opened and paramedics jumped out ordering Ted and Heath to step away.

Heath came to my side. With his arms around me to keep me warm, we watched as they labored to save Seth and Alice. When a second ambulance arrived, the victims were loaded onto gurneys and sped away.

The rest of us piled into Grandma's van and followed them to the hospital. By the time we crowded into the waiting room, Seth and Alice were in surgery. A long night awaited the rest of us.

I sat next to my crying friend and put held her hand. "He'll be fine. He's strong."

Cheryl sniffed. "I know. I just finished complaining about him being a cop." She laid her head on my shoulder.

"You weren't complaining. You were merely stating a fact."

"Coffee." Mom handed us each a cup. "We're going to need it. That, and a lot of prayer."

We sat for three hours before a doctor came to speak to us. "They are both in critical condition. We lost Miss Johnson, but were able to revive her. Officer Willis is in a medical coma. We are hopeful they will both pull through. That's all I can tell you at this time."

Two police officers marched down the hall toward us, then moved past, and took up stations in front of what I assumed was Seth's door and Alice's door.

"I suggest the rest of you head home now," the doctor said. "They won't awaken anytime soon."

Tears streamed down Cheryl's face. "Can I at least see him?"

He nodded. "Just you. Follow me."

He led her to the first room and opened the door, letting her peer into the room. After a few minutes, he put a hand on her shoulder, and said something I couldn't hear.

Cheryl shuffled toward us. "Let's find the ones who did this."

I was in total agreement. After the shock wore off and my adrenaline settled down.

~

"What's first?" Cheryl asked first thing the next morning.

"We take Mom back to finish interviewing my Dad's former coworkers. Then, once we've gathered all available information, we head to Warner." I definitely didn't want to face the Yellow Jackets without having all my facts together. I also still needed to fill the jump drive with realistically sounding information.

I turned back to my laptop and smiled. Even better, it might be better to fill the jump drive with everything we know about Sanchez. Plus, I'd make a copy. Then, if it was taken, I might have a little leverage.

"Ready?" Mom entered the cottage. "I left Grandma at the desk."

"What?" Cheryl and I said together.

"Mom, are you crazy?"

"There was no one else." She hitched her purse higher on her shoulder. "Let's go."

I grabbed my purse, closed my laptop, then followed her out after setting the alarm. Heath waited outside to lock the door.

"I'm all you have as far as security," he said. "Ida refuses to let Ted leave her side after what happened yesterday."

"You're all we need." I kissed his cheek. "I put my gun in my purse. You're welcome to use it."

He laughed. "Thanks, but Ted gave me one of his. If Seth were to find out I was carrying without a permit..." he sobered. "Well, he'd say the situation better warrant it. I think it does."

Thirty minutes later, the four of us knocked on Larry Johnson's door. I hoped he'd see us all since no one felt safe staying behind in the car.

Larry opened the door. "For crying out loud! Leave me alone." He started to close the door.

Heath stuck his foot in the way. "You might want to practice checking out who it is before opening the door."

"Charles Baker is dead. Friends of ours have been shot." Mom took a deep breath. "I need to know if there is anything you know about the son of Harvey Weston and Carmen Sanchez."

"Come in. Hurry up." He slammed the door behind us. "You're trying to get me killed. Sit down. I don't have a lot of time."

I noticed the suitcase in the corner. "Leaving?"

"Darn right, I am. Y'all have opened up Pandora's Box. I want out of here before the you-know-what hits the fan." He sat in a leather chair across from the couch.

"The Yellow Jackets are stirring, Mrs. Hart. That's never a good sign. If Baker is dead, then it's because he stopped being dirty. Yeah, we all knew. But the thing most didn't know is that he was playing both sides."

"Did my Dad ever say anything about a list of undercover agents?" I leaned forward.

"Sure, he did. Baker had one, too. His contained different names, though. Wouldn't be smart to put all the names on one list. This way, at least some of those poor guys survive." He stood. "My advice is to let this lie."

"I can't. Someone won't let it. It started the moment someone tried to kill me. What can you tell me about Harvey Weston's son?"

He grinned. "I guess you've decided to let your daughter do the talking this time, Mrs. Hart?"

"She's nicer than I am." Mom's lips curled.

"Weston's son's name was Sean. If you dig deep enough, you'll find him. The Yellow Jackets did. Now, if you'll excuse me." He grabbed his suitcase. "Have a good life." He ducked out the door and dashed to a four-wheel drive jeep in the driveway.

"That's that." Mom lifted her chin. "Just because someone resumes a new identity doesn't mean they can't be found."

"What's on your mind, Mom?"

"Let's find out who this Sean Weston is. My guess is that he's working for the Yellow Jackets in addition to getting revenge for his father. Doesn't make a lot of sense to me, since his father is dead because of his affiliation to the gang, but there's no accounting for insanity."

"Where do we look?"

Her smile widened. "If Baker was working both sides, I'm thinking he might have known something he didn't tell us. And, if he did, it might very well be hidden in the evidence room at the station. If so, it's well hidden, but I have faith we can find it. If, and it's a very big if, we can get into that evidence room."

"Where is it?"

"The station basement."

"Why would he have kept something so important?" There was no way we would be able to get into that room without Seth.

"Leverage, dear, what else? Now, hand me the copy you made so our tech guys can trace whenever a search is made online."

18

*Y*ep, no way we were getting into that room, even with Ted.

"I'm sorry, sir, but you are no longer active duty." The officer behind the screen stared without expression at Ted. "I cannot let you in. You should know that."

"I'm working on behalf of Officer Willis." Ted slapped the counter. "He's in a coma. If he could do this himself, he would."

"Without written authorization, you aren't getting in." The officer turned away, dismissing us.

"Well, that's the most ridiculous thing I've ever heard." Ted glared. "I've heard some ridiculous things while dating your grandmother, but this one takes the cake. I gave them thirty years of my life! I'd expect some courtesy."

"Now what?" I glanced around the group. "There has to be a way of finding out who Sean Weston is

155

now."

"I've one more trick up my sleeve," Ted said. "I'll contact some of the people in my past. See if they can't help me dig something up. It might take a few days, though."

I might not have a few days. I'd stayed up late last night scanning the names of police officers around the country and combining first and last names to come up with a list of my own, none of which were Arkansas law enforcement. Hopefully, should the drive be taken, it would keep the gang busy enough for a while they wouldn't have time to kill me. Since the names were real, just mixed up, it might not immediately trigger a red flag.

"How can we get the word out that I have the drive?" I asked on the way back to Grandma's van. Since the bombing, for our safety, we were allowed to park in the squad car lot.

"Leave it be. We want to stall a confrontation as long as possible," Ted said.

"I agree." Heath took my hand and squeezed. "I know you want justice, Shelby, but rushing won't accomplish that."

Mom sighed. "I have to agree with the men on this. We need to make sure we have everything in place before confronting the Yellow Jackets."

"But, we can't even look for Sean Weston." Frustration ripped through me. "We have no way of finding a person in Witness Protection, not unless we can hack FBI's computers, which we can't. I might as well go spread mulch."

I yanked open the backdoor to the van and climbed inside. I'd been involved in several murders over the last year, but none came to a screeching halt like this one.

My cell phone rang. It was Cheryl, who had decided to stay at the hospital with Seth rather than come with us. "Hey."

"I can't eat this cafeteria food one more time. Can you bring me a burger?"

"They have good burgers there."

"I need something different."

"How about a pizza?"

"Sure." Click.

"We're taking pizza to Cheryl," I said, returning my phone to my purse. As it often does when I'm idle, my mind wandered. Oddly enough to Tony Perez, aka Carmen Sanchez, and how friendly he'd been the time I met him. The man had had plenty of opportunities to grab me, kill me, etc. Everyone was right. The gang was holding back for some reason.

I straightened in my seat. Steve Olson! The new kitchen help had looked as if he'd known Tony, and he'd looked like a boy getting a glimpse of the monster under his bed. I tapped Ted on the shoulder. "Head to Shady Acres first. I want to talk to the guy in the kitchen."

Steve was the only one in the kitchen when I entered. He turned from a sink full of pans. "What's up? Joyce isn't here until later."

"It's you I want to talk to." I'd left my companions in the diningroom so we wouldn't spook the already skittish man. "Steve, when you got a look at Tony Perez, the occupant of cottage thirty-one, you looked frightened. Why?"

"His name isn't Tony Perez." He reached for a

knife on the counter.

"How do you know that?" And why did he grab a knife?

"That's none of your business." He held the knife between us.

"Put that down and answer the lady's question." Ted, gun drawn, stepped into the kitchen.

"Thanks." I moved closer to his side, glad for once he hadn't listened to my request for me to go in alone.

Steve glanced from the gun to Ted's face, then must have thought it best to comply. He set the knife on the kitchen island. "I used to live near the Yellow Jackets. I know no one is supposed to ever see the face of Sanchez, but I did…once. I was taking the garbage out at the burger joint I worked for and saw two gang members beating on some guy. Standing off to the side was Sanchez. I knew it was him because one of the guys called him by name." Steve swallowed hard, his adam's apple bobbing. "Sanchez shot him for saying his name."

"You're lucky they didn't see you," Ted said.

"I'd be dead if they had. I've never spoken of that day until now."

"We won't tell a soul," I said. "All we needed was confirmation. I don't suppose you know where we can find him?"

He shook his head. "No, but where I saw him was the corner of Madison and Greer in Warner."

"Thank you." I stepped out of the kitchen, Ted on my heels. "Do you think it's worth going there?"

He shrugged. "It is an active gang neighborhood. It makes sense that Sanchez would live around there."

The problem would be finding him without getting

ourselves killed. Oh. I just got the most brilliant idea. "Let's get that pizza. I need to talk to Cheryl."

Once again we all piled into Grandma's van and headed, first to pick up a pizza, then to deliver said pizza to Cheryl. When we arrived at the hospital, she was pacing out front.

"What took you so long? I thought maybe you had to make the sauce yourself. From scratch." She crossed her arms and tapped her foot.

"Oh, hush. Here you go." I thrust the pizza into her hands. "Eat and get happy. Then, I have a proposition for you."

"Oh, goodie." She didn't sound thrilled.

"How's Seth?"

"Still out. So is Alice, but she's showing signs of waking." Cheryl led us to an outdoor picnic table. "I know it's chilly, but they won't let us bring in outside food to eat in the cafeteria."

We shared the pizza and talked of mundane things, like how wonderful it would be to get back to normal life. The moment we finished, Cheryl wiped her mouth with a napkin and speared me with a glance.

"Spill it."

I explained our conversation with Steve. "So, I thought the easiest way to get there was to look like we fit in."

"I'm not going to like this."

"Probably not." I grinned. "Remember that one Halloween when we were twelve and you wanted to dress up as a prostitute?"

"Absolutely not. Look at me! I no longer have that body." She narrowed her eyes.

"No, there's a lot more of you to love. If we

pretend to be streetwalkers, we can go where the rest of the family can't."

"That's the dumbest idea you've ever had," Ted said. "Who's your pimp? The minute you walk onto someone else's corner, you're a target from the other girls. A good way to get yourself killed. Come up with another plan."

Well, pooh. I thought my plan was excellent. "I don't have any more ideas. We can't just waltz onto Madison and Greer."

"Why not?" Mom's eyes widened. "The whole act as if you belong thing. Ted, what is one group of people that regularly walk those streets other than prostitutes and gang members?"

He grinned. "People handing out Bible tracts. The thugs may try to intimidate, but they rarely hurt those delivering the Word of God."

"That's perfect." Grandma clapped her hands. "It won't be weird for a group this size to take a stroll."

"You'll have to dress respectable." Mom gave her 'the look'. "Not like a twenty-year-old streetwalker."

"I'll borrow an old lady dress of yours." Grandma smirked.

"Let's not get off topic," I said, then glanced at Heath. "You've been quiet this whole time. What are you thinking?"

He sighed. "I'm glad the prostitute idea fell through, for one. I know where I can get the Bible tracts, if that's what you really want to do. But, I think it better to hand over what we know to the police." He held up a hand as I opened my mouth to protest. "If you insist on going, I'll go. You know that. I said I would support you. I didn't say I had to like it. Ted, you really think we should go through with this?" His gaze switched to the older man.

"It's dangerous, I admit. But these people hide when the authorities show up. The real trick will be getting to Sanchez."

"Let's not forget about Sean Weston. The two are connected somehow," I said, gathering up the empty pizza box and napkins. "Maybe locating one of them will result in getting them both."

"In the past, you've used yourself as bait," Heath said. "Now, you want to rush headlong into the danger. I'm not sure which I dislike more."

I threw the garbage into a nearby bin, then wrapped my arms around his neck and kissed him. "It will all be fine."

"Famous last words." He returned my kiss. "What's on the agenda for the rest of the day?"

"You get the tracts, Mom and I will see what work needs done around Shady Acres, Ted is going to see if his contacts can help us find the elusive Sean, Cheryl is going to stay right here with Seth, and Grandma is going to…"

"Do whatever I want." She chuckled. "That's the benefit of being free as a bird. In fact, I think I'll get a manicure."

She had something up her sleeve, I knew it. When I tried to capture her gaze, she focused on her nails. Yep, there was definitely something cooking in the Lucille Ball red head of hers.

Grandma dropped the rest of us off at Shady Acres, then sped away with the promise to see us at supper. I wondered how effective it would be to put a trace on her phone like Heath and Ted had on mine. I felt my earlobes. Why weren't we wearing the diamond earring tracers?

I shrugged and headed to the greenhouse to make my inspection of the perimeter before actually entering the building. Once I reassured myself that all was clear, I went in and checked my drip system and the condition of my recently planted herbs. From the snipped leaves, it looked as if Joyce might have helped herself. I didn't have a problem, I grew them for the kitchen after all, but I wished she'd wait until the plants were bigger.

While I worked, I ran over what we knew about the case in my mind, which was depressingly little. Maybe I wasn't as good at solving mysteries as I'd originally thought. I'd been lucky so far. This time I was having to work for every inch I advanced. By supper time, I had a full-fledged pity party over my incompetence going on. When the bell rang, I was more than happy to have food to distract me from my thoughts.

"Shelby." Grandma waved to me from the bushes.

I frowned. "What are you doing out here? You should be inside eating."

"I went and had my nails done."

"Yeah, you told us that."

"At a shop on Madison and Greer. Oh, the things I heard."

"Tell me."

She looked so much like the Cheshire Cat she could have been the model for the fairy tale character. "The girls in the shop like to gossip, and the main topic of conversation was how the elusive Carmen Sanchez isn't so elusive anymore. He's actually been seen by a number of people. He's frantically searching for something and asking a lot of questions about you."

"Me?" My mouthed dried up.

"Of course no one in that area has ever seen, much less heard of you, so his job isn't easy. One gal said that her sister lives in Boonesville and saw Sanchez here."

"We know that. He was staying here."

Her eyes widened. "That's not all she said. She also said he's been spending a lot of time with a handsome young man she's never seen before."

Could this young man be Harvey Weston's son? "We need to find out who that man is."

19

"*W*on't the women at the salon recognize you?" I asked Grandma the next morning as we met next to her van.

"Of course, but I told them I'd be back with the Word of God, and some friends." She grinned. "I'm not an idiot, dear." She narrowed her eyes at me. "You should have worn more makeup to cover those bruises."

Ted gave her a look that could have been interpreted as not completely agreeing, but softened when she smiled his way. "We're only here to scope out the area, folks, not to engage. The only talking we do is when handing them a tract."

"Then, what's the purpose of going?" Grandma climbed into the front passenger's seat.

"To be seen and form a plan." Ted got in the driver's seat. "Contrary to what this group seems to believe, solving crime requires a lot of footwork before taking action."

"Oh, pooh." Grandma waved a hand. "That's boring."

I shared an amused glance with Heath as I scooted closer to him so Mom could get in. He took my hand and squeezed. "You clean up nice," I said, admiring him in a shirt and tie.

"So do you." His gaze ran over the simple skirt and blouse I wore under my wool coat.

Conversation ceased as we headed for Warner, thirty minutes away. I guessed they were all like me, thinking of all the things that could go wrong. I carried my weapons in my purse, and was sure Grandma and Ted were also armed, but what if we got into a gang war? What if shooting really did break out? What if…my thoughts grew wilder and wilder.

I shook my head in an attempt to clear it and stared past Heath out the window. Other than trees and other vehicles there was little to see until we hit Warner city limits. Soon, office buildings and strip malls gave way to shoddy apartments and tattoo parlors.

Ted parked on the corner of Madison and Greer. Taking a deep breath, I made sure my purse was hitched securely on my shoulder, and followed Heath from the van.

"Here are your tracts." Heath handed us each a handful. "Keep your eyes and ears open for Sanchez and men in yellow shirts or with yellow bandanas."

"Don't venture too far from the group. If you do step away," Ted said, "take someone with you. This isn't Shady Acres. There are sections of this neighborhood that not even the religious venture into."

Grandma rubbed her hands together. "Let's go!

But first, I need to pop in and say hello to my new friends."

"I'll go with her." Mom followed Grandma into Sexy Nails and More.

"What does more mean?" Heath asked.

"I don't want to know," I said. "Let's cross the street. Ted can wait for Mom and Grandma." I'd spotted someone in a yellow tee-shirt.

Side-by-side, being as sedate as possible, I pasted a smile on my face, willed my legs not to tremble and strolled down the sidewalk handing out tracts and saying how much God loved the person. This wasn't so bad. The people were actually quite polite.

Then, we turned the corner. A group of young men lounged against a graffiti-covered wall and stared with hostile eyes at us.

"I don't think we should go there," Heath said. "This street seems to be off limits to people like us."

"You mean white people?"

"I mean non-gang members." We backed up. "I think this might be one of the places Ted warned us about."

"Hey!"

We stopped.

"You here to spy on us?" One of the men marched toward us, his 'homies' right behind him. "You here to check our ranks for our enemy?"

"No." I held out a tract. "We're here to save you."

He laughed. "Do I look like I need saving? You do, though. It looks as if someone already made a mess of your face."

This must be how an animal caught in a trap felt. This man didn't want what we were handing out, and I had no idea how to approach the subject of Sanchez. So, I did the next best thing…I grabbed Heath's hand and ran. With my other hand, I fumbled in my purse for my gun.

Rushing toward us from the other direction, was the rest of our group. Behind me, I heard the slapping of gym shoes against pavement. This was a race we weren't going to win. Our friends wouldn't reach us in time and if they did, they'd be in the same danger.

Someone grabbed my purse and yanked, pulling me off my feet. They dragged me along the sidewalk. From the burning in my knees, I was certain I left skin behind.

Heath threw a punch and soon disappeared under a sea of yellow.

"Stop!" I raised my hand and fired the gun in the air. Then, climbing to my feet, I added, "The next person to move dies. Get off my fiancé."

The crowd stepped back, leaving Heath on the sidewalk.

He didn't move. Blood seeped through his jacket. By the time Ted arrived to help control the gang, I was kneeling next to the man I loved and praying the gang hadn't killed him. "Someone call an ambulance!" I pressed against what looked like a knife wound in his side. Already his handsome face was turning black and blue from the punches thrown his way.

"I ought to shoot every single one of you, "Grandma said. "There ain't nothing more dangerous than an old woman with a gun. You tell Sanchez we're looking for him. You tell him, we're coming for him. Go on. Go tell him!" She fired a shot into the ground, kicking up cement.

The crowd scattered as sirens wailed in the distance.

"Are you nuts?" Mom stood guard over me and Heath, but her words were directed toward Grandma. "Why did you tell them why we were here?"

"Because now he'll come after us." She shrugged. "Plus, it made them leave. We weren't getting out of here alive, otherwise. I watch TV. I read books."

"I hate to admit it, but Ida's right." Ted flagged down the ambulance. "Saying Sanchez's name was the most effective way to get the gang to leave."

Heath didn't stir the entire time I pressed my hands against his womb. Nor did he blink as the paramedics placed him on the gurney. Not giving them the chance to tell me I couldn't ride along, I jumped in the ambulance and glared.

They looked at each other, shrugged, and closed the door, obviously thinking it wasn't worth the battle. When we arrived at the hospital, I wasn't quite as lucky. They wheeled Heath through a set of double doors and a nurse blocked my path.

"A doctor will come talk to you as soon as we know something," she said. "You may wash up in the restroom. There's hot coffee in the waiting room. We'll take care of him to the best of our ability." She stepped back and let the doors close.

I broke into tears.

Mom put her arms around me and pulled me into the nearby lady's room. After turning on the water, she slipped my hands under the stream and washed Heath's blood from my skin.

"I'm full of stupid ideas." I sniffed. "Why did I ever think I could find Dad's killer?" I lifted my gaze to her worried one. "How can I possibly believe I can outwit a murderer? Even one that only attempted to kill me?"

"You've done it in the past, Shelby."

"By sheer dumb luck." I kicked the trashcan. "We aren't crime fighters, Mom. We're a receptionist, a gardener, a teacher, a middle-aged woman, and a retired cop. Now, Heath might be lying on an operating table dying. I can't do this anymore." I slumped to the floor.

Mom, ever present of a woman's modesty, pulled my skirt down over my knees before joining me on the cold tile. "You're right. That's all we are. But we're also a determined group to find justice and keep you alive. Doing nothing won't accomplish that."

"We're dropping like flies, Mom. First Seth and Alice, now Heath. Who's next?" No one if I had my way. Shady Acres could find another gardener easy enough. I could hide just as easy. Then, no one could find me until this whole sorry mess was behind me.

"Coffee." Grandma pushed into the room and handed me a styrofoam cup.

I took a sip. Fire burned my throat. "What's in this?"

"Whiskey. Drink it. You need it."

"Ugh." I handed the cup to Mom and leaned my head against the wall. "Is there anything you don't carry in that purse of yours?"

"Nope. Here's yours. I had to pick up most of your stuff out of the ditch, but it's all here. Except for your gun. Someone ran off with that."

I had a vague recollection of someone yanking it from my hand before racing away. "I can list it as stolen."

Why were we talking about a stolen gun when the man who holds my heart might be dying? "I'm going to sit in the waiting room."

I stepped into the hall to see Cheryl rushing toward me, arms extended. "I'm so sorry."

"Looks like we're in the same boat, huh? How's Seth?"

"Making improvement. Small, but every bit helps. I have hope." She pulled me close and held me tight. "I thought you might want to know that Alice is awake."

"I do. Can she receive visitors?"

"Yep." Cheryl linked my arm with hers and led me to Alice's room. "She's been asking to see you."

"Finally." Alice frowned as I entered. "Is that blood on your blouse?"

"It's Heath's. He was…stabbed and beaten." I plopped into the vinyl chair next to her bed. "He's in surgery. How are you feeling?"

"I was better before I knew you almost got my handyman killed."

"Not just him. The whole group. We were jumped by a gang." I rubbed my hands down my face.

"You're lucky, then. Cheryl, close the door." Ever bossy, Alice pointed.

Cheryl did as she asked. "Okay, why the secrecy?"

"Did you find my message in my office?"

"No. Now that we've found you, you can just tell us." I was tired of games.

She sighed. "Tony Perez is Carmen Sanchez. I found that out quite by accident when I heard, of all people, Scott Devine call him by his real name."

"Scott?"

"Yes, and Sanchez was not happy I can tell you

that with all certainty. In fact, he threatened Scott. Said his false identity wouldn't save him if he slipped again."

My blood must have dropped to my feet. "Scott is Sean Weston. Scott is the one who tried to kill me." Mom was going to be devastated. She'd taken the delivery man under her wing like a son.

Has he hated me the whole time we've known him? Or had he hung around when his father was a resident at Shady Acres merely to keep an eye on him? Now that Harvey was dead, it was obvious Scott, err Sean, blamed me. It also explained the ease of getting close to the greenhouse and setting it up to gas me.

"Shelby, are you listening?" Alice snapped her fingers. "Scott and Sanchez saw me listening. That's why I had to run."

"What could you have possibly left in your office to tell me all that?"

"Seriously? You call yourself a sleuth." She shook her head. "I left the number thirty-one several places. Haven't you heard of running a pencil over a desk blotter? Plus, the number was written larger than the numbers around it on several places. That should have told you that Perez wasn't who he said he was. As for Scott, Sean, whatever his name is, all you had to do was figure out the code in my black book."

The woman was nuts. "There is no way to have figured out any of that." But now that I know Scott is Sean, the fuzzy picture from Charles Baker's house does look a bit like him. That didn't come from Alice though. "You should have just sent me a text like you did before."

"Too risky."

She was hopeless. "Well, I'm not going to argue about your methods. I need to focus on Heath and confronting Scott."

20

"I heard you're looking for me?"

I glanced up from where I ate a salad in the hospital waiting room to see Carmen Sanchez, flanked by two very large men, looking down at me. A piece of lettuce stuck to the back of my throat and I choked.

Carmen pounded me on the back. When I could breathe again, he sat across from me. "It's hard to get you alone, Miss Hart."

"I try to keep it that way." I glanced toward the door.

"I won't take much of your time." He folded his hands on the tabletop. "What can I do for you?"

"Go to prison for killing my father." I sat back in my chair expecting to be shot at any second.

He looked taken aback. "I didn't kill Officer Hart, nor did I order my men to do so. Who told you this?"

"Charles Baker." I was getting very confused.

"My dear, Miss Hart. The former Officer Baker was a dirty cop. If anyone had your father killed it was him. The last thing I heard was that your father was very close to proving just how dirty Baker was."

"Then, who shot Baker?"

He shrugged. "The man had a lot of enemies. It's quite possible it was someone quite outside what is going on here."

"But there were photos of Harvey Weston and his son."

He cocked his head. "You're looking in the wrong place for the bad guy, sweetheart." His eyes glittered. "Weston and his son worked for me. Weston turned traitor. His son didn't." He planted his hands flat on the tabletop and pushed to his feet. "If I put money on who killed your father, I'd say Baker ordered the hit. Now, that man is dead. Justice has been served." He turned to go.

"Wait. Who is trying to kill me?"

He smiled. "That's an easy one that I do believe you know the answer to. Sean Weston is a bit upset over his father being sent to prison."

At least I'd figured something out. "Where can I find him?"

"He'll come to you."

I got to my feet. "Why did your men jump us?"

"It wasn't anything personal. But, when two white people approach my boys…they're a little territorial."

"They could have killed him. Or me. But they didn't even give us a chance to explain."

"Miss Hart. You're going where you shouldn't go. We're at war right now with a rival. You simply were in the wrong place at the wrong time. Now, a little birdie told me that you have a jump drive I want."

The man may not have pulled the trigger that killed my father, or Charles Baker, but he had a hand in it all. He wasn't the type to sit back and not be involved. I dug the jump drive from my pocket and slid it across the table.

"You're a doll, Miss Hart. Good day, and watch your back. Weston isn't quite all there." He tapped his temple, then led his goons out of the cafeteria.

I fell back into my seat. Charles Baker had killed my father? That would explain why Dad had approached the car. He'd known the man. My throat clogged with tears. Dad had walked willingly to a killer's side, and paid the ultimate price. Now, according to a gang boss, I was to sit back and wait for a different killer to come to me.

"What's taking you so long?" Mom rushed to my side.

"I just had a visit with Carmen Sanchez."

"What?" Shock crossed her features.

"Yeah. It was Charles Baker that killed Dad. We were so wrong on that account. Mom, we sat in his house. We watched the man get shot! All the while, he was the very one we were looking for." I didn't know what to do now that that part of my life was over. For five years I'd wanted vengeance. Now that I had it...I didn't know quite how to process it. "He also confirmed that Scott is Sean Weston and that he does want to kill me because of his father's death. He doesn't know where Sean is, but said he would come to me."

"That's a scary thought. Oh, honey, I came looking for you to tell you that Heath is out of surgery. He's asleep but is going to be just fine."

"Can I see him?"

She nodded and held out her hand for me to take. Slipping my hand in hers as I did for so many years as a child, I let her lead me to Heath's room.

"I'll be right out here if you need me," she said.

With slow steps, I approached Heath's bed. My usually strong man looked pale and helpless. The bruises on his face stood out as if painted on a white canvas. "Oh, Heath. I'm so sorry." I put my hand over his. "I shouldn't be here. You shouldn't be here. If I were brave, I'd take off the ring you gave me and give it back. I've thought about it, oh, how I've thought about it, but I can't. You have given me the hope that love is real and can last a lifetime."

His eyes fluttered open. "You've...thought...about it?"

My gaze darted to his. "Several times in a vain attempt to keep you safe."

He sighed and closed his eyes. "We'll discuss this...later. When I'm out of here. Go home and catch a killer."

Relief flooded through me so strongly I actually laughed. "Yes, I bet we will." I leaned forward and rested my head on the mattress.

When I woke, I discovered someone had draped a blanket over my shoulders and the sun was setting outside the window. I groaned and stretched. Seeing that Heath still slept, I placed a kiss on his forehead, one of the few places not sporting a bruise, then headed to see how many of my family members had stayed.

Both Mom and Grandma reclined in chairs in the waiting room. They sat up when I entered. "Where's Ted?" I asked.

"Off to find out what he could about Baker and Weston." Grandma patted the chair next to her. "How's your man?"

"He's going to be just fine." I leaned my head on her shoulder. "What do we do now?"

"Since we have to wait around for a killer," she said with a grin, "we might as well enjoy life. Alice said we've let too much time pass without a social event, and that it's time we, well you and Sue Ellen, get back to work."

Mom stood. "I guess Scott can find us there easy enough. Ready?"

"I don't want to leave Seth."

"I don't blame you," Mom said but my guess is he told you to go. Right?"

"Yes."

I stood and the three of us stepped into a chilly winter evening. In a nearby spot, Grandma's new scarlet baby waited under a streetlamp.

"Oh, goodie. Ted moved it to a closer parking spot. That man is always looking out for me." Grandma picked up the pace, then peered under the van. When she popped the hood, I knew what she was looking for.

"See anything?"

"No bombs in sight." She nodded and climbed into the driver's seat. "I do hate having to park her in public parking. So, what kind of an event should we have? It needs to be something Scott will feel comfortable crashing."

"A masquerade," I said. "But, how will we recognize him?"

"I'll know him anywhere," Mom said. "Look on his neck, below his right ear. He has a mole."

A tap on the window had us all screaming.

Cheryl beamed in at us. "Let me in. I need a shower."

"Not an enticing invitation, by any means." Grandma unlocked the door so she could join us. "I can't wait until Saturday so we can catch the little rat." Grandma pulled onto the highway. "A real man would try to kill someone face-to-face. Not tip-toe around the issue like a coward. Yep, give me a straight forward killer any day."

I'd prefer no killer, but I knew what she was trying to say. If you knew who wanted you dead, you could set a trap. Which was exactly what I planned on doing.

~

Once we got home, and we'd all enjoyed a hot shower and were now in our pajamas in my livingroom, we got down to the business of capturing a crazy person. "Do we want the masquerade to be a theme or everyone wear whatever they want?" I balanced my laptop on my lap, ready to design the flier.

"Whatever they want," Cheryl said, brushing her hair. "I'd like to see what a once Witness Protection kid, turned delivery boy, turned gang member, turned killer would choose to dress up as. It seems to me that Scott has already pretended to be a lot of things."

"Like a friend." Mom crossed her arms.

"Oh, he likes you," I said. "He's warned me several times to keep you from snooping. I just didn't know the exact reason why."

"Then I'll go with you when you confront him. He won't hurt me."

"There's no guarantee of that at this stage." I quickly typed up a flier, added some cute clipart, and sent it to the printer at the reception desk. "It's waiting for distribution. The trick will be letting Scott know. He won't exactly be delivering copy paper anymore."

"We'll tack them all over the grounds," Cheryl said. "He's bound to be watching you."

I shuddered and glanced at the window. Sure enough, a pair of eyes peered in. It took me a moment to realize Scott wouldn't be so obvious. I opened the front door. "Leroy, what have I said about peeking in my window?"

"I thought you might want to know that Scott was hanging around your cottage last night. I ran him off, but he looked as if he was up to no good. Now, considering all that's been happening with you, why don't you have a man in there?"

"We're waiting on Ted," Grandma yelled. "Go back to your coffin."

"I'm sorry, Leroy. She's rude." I tossed Grandma a glare.

"It's nuts how he can't go in the sunlight."

Leroy laughed, bared his teeth, and set off to continue his night time prowling.

"Don't be mean to my friends, Grandma." I locked the door. "Where exactly is Ted?"

"Working in the report room at the police station. He said he'd be here before too late." She studied her nails. "Those girls did a good job. Too bad I can't go back there after creating a scene on the street."

"Ignore her," Mom said. "We have planning to do. What costume are you going to wear, Shelby?"

"I think I'll go as Nancy Drew." All I'd need was a red wig and an old-fashioned dress which I knew I could find in Grandma's closet.

"I'll go as Beth." Cheryl grinned. "I'm a big Beth, but that's okay."

"I'm going as Marilyn Monroe," Grandma said.

"You always do." Mom frowned.

"It suits me."

Mom rolled her eyes. "Lucille Ball would be better."

"Or Lady Godiva." Grandma wiggled her eyebrows.

We all groaned.

It didn't really matter what we dressed as. The important thing was that we went, we stayed alert, and we caught the man trying to kill me. That last part might not be so easy. I'd need to buy a new gun by Saturday. Maybe I could stop on my way to the hospital to see Heath in the morning. I'd also have to pick up some decorations, then talk to Joyce about food. It was good to return to a semblance of normalcy, if only for a few days.

I had three days until Scott and I had a showdown.

21

*S*aturday arrived with Ted not having found out much more than we already knew. Scott was Sean Weston. The new bit of information was that Sean had spent time under a psychiatrist's care as a young teen. But, the records were sealed.

So, it was a very sour-faced Keystone cop who arrived to pick up Nancy Drew, her sidekick Beth, and an aging Marilyn Monroe. Mom dressed as Mother Goose.

"I'm not feeling very social," Ted growled. "So, this punk better show up."

Grandma giggled. "If you're going to talk like that then you should have come as Dirty Harry."

"Let's not forget why we're having this get-together," Mom said. "It's not only for the residents to socialize. We're on a dangerous mission."

My mother, the voice of reason. "Keep your wits

about you, and someone stay close to me. I don't think he'll kill me if I'm surrounded by people." At least I hoped not.

I slipped my phone into an inside pocket of the suit jacket I wore. I took a deep breath and squared my shoulders. "Let's get this over with."

As expected, we arrived in the dining room ahead of the crowd. Joyce, dressed as a chef, which considering that's what she was, wasn't much of a change except her hat was taller than usual, had outdone herself with a marvelous spread of appetizers. She stood behind the buffet and grinned. "Bonjour! I'm a French chef."

I laughed. "This looks wonderful."

"I take great pride in my work." Her face beamed.

As was expected of the event's coordinator, I stood and welcomed the guests as they arrived. Most were easily recognizable, but a few were in complete costume and wore masks. One of them had to be Scott. I pointed them out to the others and continued on as if I weren't about to face my attacker.

Someone put old-tyme band music on a record player and the residents lined up for the buffet. It looked as if everyone had chosen to attend and every seat was taken. Wonderful. All of Shady Acres would witness my demise.

Bob Satchett swung Mom onto a cleared bit of floor for a dance. A smile lit up her face. Putting an end to the question of who had killed my father eased the tension from her features. She was ready to move on. I couldn't think of a better man for her than Bob. Her softness smoothed his rough edges.

But, oh, how I missed Heath. It wasn't a party

without my hero beside me.

"You're supposed to look happy," Grandma said, handing me a plate with won tons, spring rolls, chicken wings, and potato skins. "I know your sweetie isn't here, but you shouldn't look as if you're expecting Scott."

"But I am." I stared at the variety of food on my plate. This was one of the rare times I had no appetite.

"Eat up. If he abducts you, you'll need your strength." She patted me on the shoulder and sashayed away, her white dress flirting with her knees. She must have driven the men wild when she was young. Now, she only tormented Ted.

"Stop looking at everyone as if you don't expect to see them again." Cheryl stood next to me, her plate full.

"Why is everyone so worried about how I look?" I stuffed a won ton in my mouth. Seriously, didn't I have the right to look how I wanted?

"People are asking what's wrong with you. If I tell them the truth, you'll have a circle so tight around you not even your mother could get close."

True. Most of the residents adored me. I grinned. "They love me because I throw parties and keep the place looking pretty."

"Whatever. You know your poker buddies would storm the gates of Hades for you. Even that weird vampire guy. I'm going to go scout the room and see if I can locate Scott. Maybe we can take him off guard rather than the other way around."

I nodded. That would be amazing. For the first time since arriving in this retirement community, I would have the upper hand with the bad guy.

"May I have this dance?" Ted held out his hand. "I

can see you need a strong shoulder right now."

"I do. Thank you." I stepped into a waltz with him, grateful for the distraction. "Who's in charge of the music?"

"Anyone and everyone. There's a stack of vinyls that covers just about every era. When one record stops, someone puts on another."

"Good idea." Why have one person miss the party to man the music? "I feel as if I'm wasting my time standing around. I want to approach the five masked men and find out which one is Scott."

"What if none of them are?"

"What if one of them is?"

He laughed. "We're at a standstill, I see." He stepped back and bowed. "The best way to get a man to open up at a party is to hand him a drink. Since we don't really want drunks here, why not ask them to dance?"

"Good idea." It would allow me to be proactive.

With a smile on my face, I approached the first of the masked men, someone pretending to be Bill Clinton. Seriously, how many men at Shady Acres had the same physical build as Scott? There had to be a twenty to thirty year difference in age. Still, most who lived here kept in physical shape. I wasn't going to let a little bias such as age stop me from getting closer to them. It would be easy enough for Scott to put a slump in his shoulders.

"Would you like to dance?"

"Sure, Shelby." Harold Ball dragged me onto the floor.

After several minutes of a rowdy polka of some kind, he spun me and let me go. I stumbled into a table full of plastic flutes. The beautiful pyramid Grandma had set up toppled to the floor. Thank goodness they weren't glass.

"Harvey Ball!" Grandma glared at him. "That took me hours to set up."

He pulled off his mask. "I'm sorry, Ida, but it's hard to see wearing this thing. I'll pick them up." He painfully got to his knees.

"Get up, you old fool," Grandma said. "I'll have the kitchen staff help me. You'll put your back out."

Relief fluttered across his face as he got back to his feet. "I guess I got a little excited to dance with a pretty girl." He tossed me a wink. "Are you all right, Shelby?"

"I'm just fine. Don't worry about it." I was already scoping out my next dance partner. There, in the corner, Barack Obama, wearing a mustard yellow jute suit. I laughed. There was no way Scott would be caught in that getup. Still, I had to eliminate all possibilities.

"Dance?"

"Nope." A gruff voice came from behind the mask. "These old knees can't handle such activities."

His voice almost sounded as if he were faking the gravelly sound. I shifted, trying to see behind his right ear.

"What are you doing? Go away. I prefer being left alone."

"But it's a party. If you don't like people, why did you come?" I just couldn't get a good look. The man wore a terrible gray wig that fit poorly and covered part of his ears.

"You're nosy. Go away. I like watching people make fools of themselves like you did with the wine glasses. Hilarious."

I stepped back and studied him. "You're one of the new residents, aren't you?"

He groaned. "Theodore Beale."

"Have a good evening." So, Theo wasn't the one I was looking for. I had three more masked men to target.

I chose the gorilla. "Want to dance?"

"In this costume? Are you crazy?" Officer Wayman's voice, although muffled, came through the hole in the mouth. "Since Seth is out of commission, I got stuck with the job of attending this party and couldn't be recognized. I'm hot, I'm itchy, and I'm hungry."

"I could bring you a plate and you could duck into the kitchen to eat," I offered. "You'd be able to see me if you part the sliding window, but could be free to take off your mask."

"That's the best thing I've heard all day. Will you help?"

"Definitely." I filled his plate with a taste of everything and carried it to the kitchen where a very sweaty Officer Wayman sat at the island. "I should have come as a ghost or something."

I pressed my lips together to keep from laughing. The poor thing. "You'll get used to being inconvenienced if you hang around here long enough." I patted his furry shoulder and headed out to find my next victim.

By the time I danced and found out the last two masked men weren't Scott either, I started to think the crazy man wasn't coming. I plopped into a chair and took off my black pumps. Why did Nancy Drew have to be from a prior era where women dressed up when they left the house? Or, I could have come as a gardener, I suppose, with overalls and my pretty black and white rain boots. Why hadn't I thought of that?

"Soak them in Epsom salts tonight." Grandma plopped into the chair next to me. "I've got quite the stash from wearing heels all the time." She held out her leg. "And killer calves."

I laughed. "That you do. I've danced until my feet want to fall off and haven't found Scott. He isn't here."

"He'll probably grab you on your way home." She took a sip of her wine.

"Why do you have to make me more scared than I already am?"

"Fear keeps you alert. That's how I stay thin. I'm terrified of getting fat. It makes me watch everything I put in my mouth."

"It's not quite the same thing." I glanced to the pass-through from the kitchen to the dining room. "The police department sent Wayman to watch over things here. He's the big gorilla."

"I did notice him. That's who I pegged to be Scott." She set her glass down. "Well, I've some dancing left in me and that Birdie and Hattie are eye-balling my man. Ciao."

Since Alice wasn't here to yell at me for sitting around, I kept my shoes off and chose to watch the partiers rather than participate. Mom had eyes for no one but Bob, Grandma was laughing at something Ted said, and I was again missing my love.

I stood and grabbed my shoes. Swinging them from my fingers, I joined my family. "I'm going to have Officer Wayman walk me home. I'm done."

Ted nodded. "Make sure he does. If he can't, come and get me. Under no circumstances are you to walk alone."

"Understood." I glanced around for the gorilla. No sign up him, so I headed for the kitchen. No big monkey. Well, I suppose even he would have to visit the men's room.

I leaned against the wall in the short hallway and waited. When he came from the bathroom, I straightened. "About time. You take as long as a woman. I'm ready to go home and I need an escort. Can you walk me?"

He nodded.

"Great. We'll duck out the backdoor. I've already told my family I was leaving." I shoved open the door and shivered as a blast of cold air hit me. "I should have brought a jacket. I bet you aren't cold in that costume."

"Not a bit, Shelby Hart." A gun pressed against my kidney.

22

I froze. "You aren't Officer Wayman. What did you do to him?"

"He's knocked out in the bathroom. I'm not stupid enough to kill a cop. You, on the other hand, I'm willing to take my punishment." Scott did not sound like the nice, kind of shy delivery man I'd known. He really did sound like Sean, the son of Harvey.

"Head for the parking lot. I have the infamous white panel van parked there. Isn't that what all men like me use?"

I tried to swallow against a mouth suddenly filled with cotton, but my mouth was like the deadlands. Wrong choice of words. I nonchalantly dropped one shoe as we rounded the corner of the building and the other at the edge of the parking lot. At least those looking for me would know we'd left by vehicle.

Scott shoved me inside the van. "Hold out your

hands."

"No."

He aimed the gun at my head. "Do it."

"You're going to kill me anyway, why not here?"

He pulled off the gorilla head and tossed it in back with me. "This is not where you're supposed to die. Now hold. Out. Your. Hands. If you don't, I'll march back in there and shoot your crazy grandmother."

I held out my hands and cried out as he wrapped a zip tie around them.

Sean, I could no longer think of him as Scott, slammed the door closed. After he climbed into the driver's seat, he unzipped the costume and pulled it down to his waist. Then, he started the van and rocketed from the parking lot.

Rolling around like a can of vegetables that had fallen from a grocery sack, I wrapped my arms around the gorilla head in an attempt to provide some cushioning to my already sore body. Plus, the fur on the head gave me a little warmth when I shoved my bound hands inside.

"Where are we going?"

"None of your business."

"It kind of is, if you're going to leave my body there." I tried to get to my knees. If I could get the gorilla head over his head, then he'd be blind and run us into a ditch. Then, I could escape. I'd used this same ruse before to success. Only, I didn't use a gorilla head. I used my hands. And I wasn't alone. Cheryl had been with me.

I decided not to chance getting into a physical altercation with my hand tied and instead, curled up on a pile of oily smelling rags. Not to sleep, I was too frightened to do that, but because cold was quickly creeping into my bones. Of course, Scott would pick the coldest night of the year to kidnap me. To add insult to injury, both Heath and Seth were in the hospital and unable to rescue me as was the norm. I was completely on my own. Which did not bode well for me.

I raised up to peer over the driver's seat. A straight stretch of highway was in front of us. Trees on both sides. It looked like most of the stretches of highway in Arkansas.

Sean turned the wheel sharply to the right, taking us down a narrow road and me to the floor. I fell on something hard and groaned.

My phone. I smiled. Heath had installed a tracker. My family would know where I was. Relief at knowing I wouldn't stay alone filled me and quickly died upon realizing it would take them time to notice I was missing. Until they returned to my cottage to go to sleep, they wouldn't know.

"What time is it?"

"Eight."

They might not leave the party until at least ten, then they had to clean up. I had to stay alive for three hours. I fell back onto the oily rags.

"It isn't my fault your father was killed in prison," I said. "He was the murderer. He was the one who turned against the gang. The very gang you now work for, to be precise. How can you do that?"

"If you hadn't have meddled in something that didn't concern you, he wouldn't have gone to prison. As for the gang, they're just a way to get what I need. Sanchez has great ideas for killing people. The gas carbon monoxide was his idea. Genius."

"Not really. It's overdone in my opinion."

"What do you know?" He slammed on the brakes, sending me smashing into the back of his seat. Then, he pressed hard on the gas, sending me rolling in the other direction.

"I miss Scott." I wiped my face on my shoulder, suspecting I'd busted my lip.

"Scott never existed."

"Too bad. He was nice."

He stopped and started the van a few more times until I really thought I might puke.

"Stop acting like a child!" I tossed the gorilla head at him. It bounced off the front window and into his face.

This time when he stopped the van, it was so he could reach back and smack me.

I scurried out of reach.

He picked up his gun from where he'd placed it in the passenger seat. Really? How had I not known that? I could have tried to take it. "Stop fooling around or I'll shoot you."

I made a face and sat back. Not because I believed he would shoot me, he'd said the van wasn't the place I'd die, but because I was exhausted.

"I'm glad the gang didn't kill you," he said. "I wouldn't have the pleasure then."

"If you're not really a member, they'll kill you. I hope I'm there to see it."

"I don't know how sweet Sue Ellen could have raised a woman like you. I kind of thought of her as the mother I can't remember. I really hope my mother had been as kind."

"Probably not, considering how you turned out."

He zig-zagged the wheel.

I struck my head against the wall panel. I really needed to shut up before I got knocked out or my rolling around broke my phone. I prayed it hadn't.

"Did you kill Charles Baker?"

"Yep."

I turned my head and stared at the back of his. "Why?"

"Because he made your mother sad."

This guy had an unhealthy fixation on my mother. Eew.

I'd seen a video once of a girl getting free of zip ties by using the laces of her gym shoes. Well I didn't have the shoes or the laces, but I did have the edge of a gorilla head. If I rubbed hard enough and fast enough on the plastic edge, it was bound to cut into my bindings. I set to work like a mad woman, not looking up until we stopped again.

Uh-oh. Not the graveyard. I now recognized where we were.

High ornate wrought-iron fences rose in front of us. Sean was going to kill me in the place his father's body lay. I hated graveyards. Not that I was afraid of ghosts, not really. They didn't exist, I didn't think. But I had a very active imagination that tended to veer in crazy directions when among the resting places of the dead.

"Not afraid of ghosts, are you?" Sean asked, pulling me from the van.

"No, just the living." I yanked away from him.

He glanced at my feet. "Where are your shoes? Did you leave them as a trail to follow?" He bopped me in the back of the head. "Now, you'll have to walk across a gravel path in bare feet."

"I was out of bread crumbs. So, where do they bury the killers?"

"You'll find out." He grabbed my arm again and forced me to keep up with his brisk pace.

Sharp rocks dug into my bare feet. At this rate, I wouldn't be able to run if I did get away.

"Wait. Stop. I need to rest." I leaned against a tombstone.

"Nope. I've an agenda to keep. It's not my fault you thought you'd be clever and drop your shoes."

"As Scott, you didn't talk much. I liked you better then."

"So you've said." He shoved me ahead of him.

My hands parted a bit. I peered through the dark to see that I'd almost succeeded in sawing through the zip tie. One good pull and I'd be free. Now, to find the perfect opportunity to bolt. I needed a distraction.

"We've a bit of a ways to go," he said. "Dad is buried in the far corner. I guess that's where they put murderers. Like you. I have the perfect spot picked out for you. No one will discover your body until they dig the ground back up to put someone's Aunt Betsy."

"Or Uncle Harvey."

He jabbed the gun into my back. "Don't mention my father's name."

I shrugged. I guessed we had a bit of double standards here. He could talk creepily about my mother, but I couldn't mention his father even while telling the truth.

"Here we are."

We stopped in front of a newly dug, shallow grave. The simple marker on the plot next to it stated Harvey

Weston, Beloved Father, Gone to Soon. It should have said crazed killer of an even crazier son.

I glanced around us, desperately looking for a distraction. One bullet and I'd be getting buried.

"You don't have to do this, Sean. You can just walk away. Disappear again. Sanchez will help you get a new identity."

He shook his head. "I've been planning this moment for too long to walk away now. I've dreamed of killing you, Shelby. Oh, I thought we could be friends...once. Before you caught my father. He was only protecting himself, you know. Aren't we allowed to protect ourselves?"

"You seem to be denying me that right." I stared into his eyes. I'd never seen such dead eyes before. How had I not noticed. Then, the moon hid behind the clouds again and his features were shadowed.

I wanted to beg for my life. To tell him how he'd make my mother sad. How she'd probably hunt him down until her dying day, but I couldn't Pride would always be something I couldn't shed. I could not tell him any of that, so I chose to say nothing. Instead, I stared defiantly.

"What?"

I said nothing.

"Don't stare at me like that, say something!"

I heaved a sigh.

"I'll kill you right now."

What was he waiting for? Did he want me to beg? Could I prolong his plans by not speaking? It was worth a try.

I shivered violently, the cold starting to sap my strength. I'd have to make my move soon. I stomped my feet to get the blood circulating.

"What are you doing? Is that some kind of death dance?" Sean lifted the gun and aimed at my head. "Stop it. What are you looking at?"

"What is that?" I narrowed my eyes and looked over Sean's shoulder.

"What?" He turned.

"Zombies!" I yanked my hands apart, shoved Sean into the hole in the ground meant for me, and ran.

23

I had no idea why I yelled out zombies. It's the first thing that came to my adled brain. What was scarier than a crazy man with a gun? The walking dead. At least to me.

"I am going to kill you slowly!" Sean's words carried across the night air.

It wouldn't take him long to climb out of the hole. I needed a place to hide. There, behind a towering marble angel with wings spread. Maybe she could protect me.

With my back plastered to the marble base, I pulled out my cell phone. Of course there was no service. The dead didn't need cell phone service. Still, I typed a text to Ted telling him where I was and pressed send. Hopefully, I'd hit upon a hot spot as I tried to outrun Sean.

"Ollie ollie oxen free," Sean sang.

How could I not have known a year ago that this man was a few matches short of a full box? He'd even fooled Mom, and that was no easy task.

As his voice grew louder, signifying he was moving closer, I scurried to another stone, then a tree. As he moved even closer, I burrowed into a pile of leaves, leaving only a peep hole. Thank you, God, for whatever landscape crew didn't finish their job. Not only was I a bit warmer, but I was hidden.

Sean stomped past me cursing. He stopped so close to my hiding place I could have reached out and touched his ankle.

I held my breath, releasing it slowly as he moved past.

"I will find you, Shelby Hart. I know you're in here." A rock bounced into the leaves covering me. More curses filled the air, and Sean moved away.

When sleep threatened to overtake me, I knew the time had come to move. I might be warmer than out of the leaves, but hypothermia could still set in. I was dressed in a cheap polyester woman's suit and no shoes. I had no choice.

I slowly sat up and peered around. Not an easy task with cloud cover thickening. Oh, please, don't let it rain. I'd die of pneumonia.

Not seeing Sean, I got to my feet, every bone and muscle protesting at the movement. Still, I knew the importance of moving when temperatures dropped.

A shot rang out, kicking up the leaves where I'd lain.

I took off in the opposite direction, doing my best to zig-zag as I'd seen actors do in the movies. I stopped for a couple of seconds against a tree to catch my breath, then continued on until the fence stopped by mad dash through the graveyard. There had to be another way in and out of here other than the front gate.

Another shot came so close, it tugged at my hair. I realized I might not get out of this confrontation alive. My steps faltered. No. I'd fight until the end.

I scanned the wrought iron fence. There was no way to climb over the sharp peaks at the top. I'd have to find a back way or make my way to the front gate. As my body wore down, both ways seemed more impossible as the minutes ticked away from me.

"Let's stop this nonsense," Sean said, stepping from behind a tree. "You know how this must end. I'm cold, I'm tired, and I have things to do. Like move to Mexico. There is one thing that might keep me from killing you, though."

"What?" I leaned over and fought to breathe.

"That jump drive. If I had it, I could sell it to Sanchez, at great risk to my life, of course. But it would provide me extra funds to start my new life."

"He already has it."

He scowled. "That is unfortunate. Turn around and get on your knees."

I straightened, looking him in the eyes. "I will not. If you want to shoot me, Sue Ellen's only daughter, then you will do it looking at me."

The hand holding the gun shook.

My mother was his weakness and the only chance I had of staying alive. "You say you care for her, that she's the mother you can't remember. Would you kill her only child? Just go, Sean. Go to Mexico and start a new life. Just let us be."

"I can't. I need retribution. You took away the only

family member I had."

"He killed people, Sean. Innocent people." I wrapped my arms around my middle in a vain attempt to keep from freezing. "You know what? Just shoot me. I'm freezing to death anyway. Just make sure to attend my funeral somehow so you can see what you did to my mother."

"Scott!" My mother's voice had never sounded so sweet...or so terrifying. What if her being here resulted in not only my death, but hers?

Sean turned his head, but kept the gun trained on me. "You shouldn't be here, Sue Ellen."

"Of course, I should." She stopped a few feet from him. "Hand over the gun, son. There's no way you're leaving here otherwise." She glanced at me.

I nodded and fell to my knees, desperately wanting my pile of leaves. Keeping my eye on Mom and Sean, I curled into a ball and fought to keep from falling asleep.

"Let me take her home." Mom held a hand out to me. "I'll make sure she's punished for her crimes as any good mother disciplines her child. You go on now."

He blinked and shook his head. "I—" He whipped around as Ted and Officer Wayman stepped into view.

"Drop it, son," Officer Wayman ordered. "You're outnumbered."

Sean frowned. "How did you find us? I planned this so carefully. It was foolproof."

I laughed. "You forgot to check me for a phone. A simple mistake ruined your plan."

Sean's shoulders slumped. He dropped his gun, then fell to his knees, putting his hands behind his head. "I know the drill."

While Wayman handcuffed Sean, Ted put his jacket around my shoulders and helped me to my feet. "Come on, sweetie. Let's get you warmed up."

Waiting outside the front gate was a heated squad car and thick quilted houseshoes. I slipped my feet into them and cried from relief. I wasn't going to die today. I glanced up at Ted. "What took you so long?"

"No signal." He gave a sad smile. "I was scared this time, little girl."

"Yeah, me, too." I'd been scared before, but this time I'd been alone.

Mom slid into the backseat with me. "Let's have her checked out at the hospital, Ted. Officer Wayman is handling Scott."

"Did you have words with him?" I asked.

"Not really." She sighed. "I told him I felt sorry for how misled he was. The poor thing has issues, Shelby. He needs help."

"Well, maybe he'll get that help in prison. That's as far as my charitable thoughts will go right now."

~

At the hospital, the doctor wasn't too concerned about my exposure to the cold since I was warming up quite nicely. He even let me sit in Heath's room while I drank a cup of hot coffee.

"I'm sorry I wasn't there to save you," Heath said. "I like being your knight in shining armor."

"This time you had to be my wounded knight in a hospital gown." I grinned over the rim of my cup. "But, you did save me, in a way. If not for the tracking device on my phone, Ted would never have gotten there in time."

His caring gaze caressed my face. "I still would

have liked to have been the one to be there for you."

"Hopefully, you won't have to again. I can't help but wonder when my luck will run out."

He chuckled. "You can't stay away, Shelby. It's an addiction. No matter how much you say you won't get involved again, something makes it popular and off you go. I don't think the Shady Acres Gumshoes will stop anytime soon."

Ted strolled into the room, a huge grin on his weathered face. "You did it again, Shelby Hart. Your made-up list of names led us right to Sanchez's hangout. We arrested him and several members of his gang."

"Great. Another dangerous man mad at me."

"This one thinks you're outstanding. He said if he could find another woman as smart and conniving as you, he'd marry her."

"I'm glad she's mine." Heath sat up further in bed. "I'm going to marry her and get her pregnant right after so she'll stop this running around."

Ted laughed. "I doubt even being pregnant will stop this gal."

24

One month later

"*Y*ou look beautiful, Grandma." I stood in the doorway of her cottage and admired the peacock blue dress she wore. A sheath dress with a bodice and sleeves of lace. On her head was perched a hat, with a peacock feather, and a small lacy veil that fell over her eyes. "I can't believe you're getting married."

She smiled at me in the mirror. "It's about time for you to set your wedding date, dear. Heath might not wait forever."

"He won't have to." I was going to marry my man…someday. Just not right now. I was still smarting over my ex dumping me at the altar, then getting himself killed by his latest.

Grandma made a slight adjustment to the placement of her feather, then turned. "I hope to have another mystery for us to solve when I return from Bora Bora."

"I'm hoping for a few month's reprieve." I shook my head. "You're incorrigible."

"It keeps me young." She patted my cheek. "Now, where's that man of yours? He's giving me away." She dug in a small box on her dresser then pinned a white silk rose to the bodice of the light blue cocktail dress I wore.

Mom and I were standing in as maids of honor. Luckily, since Grandma insisted on an outdoor wedding, the weather cooperated, gracing us with a high of fifty-seven.

"There's the two most beautiful women in Arkansas." Heath, looking way too sexy in a black tuxedo, stood in the doorway. "The groom is getting restless."

"If he looks half as good in his tux as you do, then I'm one lucky lady." Grandma linked her arm with his. "I'm almost tempted to dump Ted and turn cougar if it meant hooking up with you."

"Hands off." I playfully slapped her arm. "He's mine."

Mom waited for us next to the pool, wearing a dress identical to mine. Bob placed a tender kiss on her cheek, then left, presumably to stand with Seth as best men. From the other side of the hedge, I could hear the murmurs of the residents gathered to witness the nuptials. If my guess was right, all of Shady Acres was in attendance.

I stepped onto the sidewalk, Mom behind me,

Grandma and Heath behind her as a recording of the wedding march sounded. Smiling, I started the tiny step march toward the rose covered arch next to the fountain.

Seth, looking none the worse for wear, stood next to a beaming-faced Ted. Next to him stood a fidgety Bob. Interesting. Did weddings make him nervous?

Cheryl sat in the front row, grinning as I strolled by. "You're next," she called out.

My face heated. I wanted to throw the roses I held in my hand at her head. Instead, I took my place next to the altar and turned. I know it was Grandma's big day, but my gaze stayed locked on Heath. I was a lucky girl.

"End of May, Heath! I'll marry you the end of May."

His grin was all the answer I needed.

"Stop the wedding." Grandma marched next to Ted. "If Shelby is getting married in May, then I say Teddy and I postpone and have a double ceremony." She grinned at me. "Won't that be super special, Shelby?"

Ted's mouth dropped open before he dissolved in a fit of laughter.

The End

Scan the code to learn about Vine Entrapment, the final installment of the Shady Acres series.

ABOUT THE AUTHOR

Multi-published and Amazon Best-Selling author Cynthia Hickey had three cozy mysteries and two novellas published through Barbour Publishing. Her first mystery, Fudge-Laced Felonies, won first place in the inspirational category of the Great Expectations contest in 2007. Her third cozy, Chocolate-Covered Crime, received a four-star review from Romantic Times. All three cozies have been re-released as ebooks through the MacGregor Literary Agency, along with a new cozy series, all of which stay in the top 50 of Amazon's ebooks for their genre. She had several historical romances release in 2013, 2014, 2015 through Harlequin's Heartsong Presents, and has sold half a million copies of her works. She has taught a Continuing Education class at the 2015 American Christian Fiction Writers conference. She is active on FB, twitter, and Goodreads, and is a contributor to Cozy Mystery Magazine blog and Suspense Sisters blog. She and her husband run the small press, Forget Me Not Romances, which includes some of the CBA's well-known authors. She lives in Arizona with her husband, one of their seven children, two dogs, two cats, three box turtles, and two Sulcata tortoises. She has seven grandchildren who keep her busy and tell everyone they know that "Nana is a writer". Visit her website at www.cynthiahickey.com

www.ingramcontent.com/pod-product-compliance
Lightning Source LLC
Chambersburg PA
CBHW070257120726
47910CB00007B/2286